**LARGE
PRINT**

EVA

Evans, Richard Paul

The Noel stranger

10/16/2019

THE
NOEL STRANGER

Center Point
Large Print

Also by Richard Paul Evans and available from Center Point Large Print:

The Mistletoe Promise
The Mistletoe Inn
The Mistletoe Secret
The Noel Diary

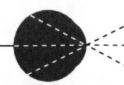

**This Large Print Book carries the
Seal of Approval of N.A.V.H.**

THE *NOEL* STRANGER

RICHARD PAUL EVANS

CENTER POINT LARGE PRINT
THORNDIKE, MAINE

This Center Point Large Print edition
is published in the year 2019 by arrangement with
Simon & Schuster, Inc.

Copyright © 2018 by Richard Paul Evans.

The text of this Large Print edition is unabridged.
In other aspects, this book may vary
from the original edition.
Printed in the United States of America
on permanent paper.
Set in 16-point Times New Roman type.

ISBN: 978-1-64358-346-4

The Library of Congress has cataloged this record
under Library of Congress Control Number: 2019944750

To Keri 2.0

CHAPTER
One

You might be wondering why I would let you, a complete stranger, read parts of my diary. Maybe it's the "bus-rider syndrome," in which people, for unknown reasons, share with total strangers the most intimate details of their lives. Maybe, but I think it's simpler than that. I think our desire to be understood is stronger than our fear of exposure.

—Maggie Walther's Diary

How did I get here?

I once heard someone describe her life as a car with four flat tires. I would be happy with that. If my life were a metaphorical car, it would be in much worse shape—wheels stolen, windshield smashed, and dirt poured into its gas tank. I'd say that the demolition of my life happened in a matter of months, but that's not really true. It had been happening for the last three years of my marriage. I was just oblivious.

You probably read about the horror of my life in the newspaper or somewhere online. It's one of those tragic stories that people love to wring their hands over and feign sympathy about as they lustfully share the sordid details—like describing a car accident they witnessed.

Before the truth popped out like a festering pustule (excuse the gross simile, it just seems fitting), my life seemed idyllic on the surface. I own a thriving—and exhausting—catering company called Just Desserts. (We do more than desserts. The woman I inherited the business from started by baking birthday and wedding cakes, and the name stuck.)

My husband of nine years, Clive, whom, by the way, I was madly in love with, was a partner in a prominent Salt Lake City law firm and a city councilman going on almost four years. I went through the whole campaign thing with him twice, speaking to women's groups, holding babies, the whole shebang. It wasn't really my thing, I've always been more of an introvert, but it was his and I loved him and believed in supporting my husband. Unlike me, Clive was a natural at public life. Everyone loved him. He had a way of making you feel like you were the most important person in the room. I think that's what initially drew my heart to him—the way he made me feel seen.

Less than a year ago, Clive's name had been placed on the short list of potential Salt Lake City mayoral candidates for next year's election. One newspaper poll even showed him leading, and lobbyists and politicos began circling him like bees at a picnic. At least they were. No one's calling now. That ship didn't sail, it sunk. Just like our marriage.

I've learned that the things that derail our lives are usually the things that blindside us when we're worrying about something else—like stressing over being late to a hair appointment and then, on the way there, getting T-boned by a garbage truck running a red light.

My garbage truck came via a phone call at nine o'clock on a Tuesday morning. Clive was out of town. I had just gotten home from a Pilates class and was getting ready for work when the phone rang. The caller ID said *Deseret News*, the local newspaper. I assumed the call had something to do with our subscription or my catering business, as the paper would call every now and then for a food article. Last Halloween they had me do a bit on "Cooking for Ghouls," sharing my favorite chili and breadstick recipe.

I picked up the phone. "Hello?"

"Mrs. Walther?"

"Yes."

"I'm Karl Fahver, the political editor for the *Deseret News*. I'm calling to see if you'd like to comment on your husband's arrest this morning."

My heart stopped. "What are you talking about?"

"You didn't know that your husband was arrested this morning?"

"My husband's away on a business trip. I have no idea what you're talking about."

"I'm sorry, I assumed you knew. Your husband was arrested for bigamy."

"Bigamy? As in, more than one wife?"

"Yes, ma'am."

My mind spun like that beach-ball-looking thing on your computer when you're waiting for something to happen. Or maybe I was just in shock. "That's ridiculous. I'm his only wife. Are you sure you have the right person?"

The reporter hesitated. When he spoke again, there was a hint of sympathy in his voice. "According to the police report, your husband has a second family in Colorado."

Just then my call waiting beeped. It was Clive. "My husband's on the other line. I need to get this . . ."

"Mrs. Walther—"

I hung up, bringing up Clive's call. "Is it true?" I asked.

Clive didn't answer.

"Clive . . ."

"I'm sorry, Maggie. I wanted you to hear it from me."

"You wanted me to hear from you that you have another wife?" I started crying. "How could you do this?!"

Nothing.

"Answer me!"

"What do you want me to say, Maggie?"

"Say it's not true! Say, 'I'd never do this to the woman who supported me through everything.' How about, 'I'd never do this to you because I love you'?" There was another long pause. I couldn't stop crying. Finally, I said, "Say something, please."

"I'm sorry," he said. "I've got to go." He hung up.

I collapsed on the floor and sobbed.

According to the article in the afternoon's paper, my husband had another wife and two children in Thornton, Colorado. I saw a picture of the other woman. She was short, with a round face, a tattoo of a rose on her shoulder, and badly dyed blond hair.

After the story went viral, a malicious site popped up showing a picture of me next to the "other wife" and asking people to vote which one was hotter. There were more than twelve thousand votes. I won, 87 percent to 13 percent. I'm sorry I know that. It should have at least preserved my ego a little, but it only made me angrier. Clive could at least have had the decency to cheat on me with a swimsuit model—someone no one would really expect a normal woman to compete with. One that would have people saying, "I can see him doing that," instead of "His wife must have been awful to live with."

At the moment, Clive's out on bail, living

with his parents in Heber, Utah. I doubt with his connections that he'll ever see the inside of a cell—unless he ends up with a judge he's crossed somewhere back—but either way, I'm feeling like I'm under house arrest, afraid to go out in public, even to shop for groceries. I'm afraid to see strangers gape at me.

The other day I went to the nearby food mart to pick up something to eat when I noticed a woman following me. At first I told myself that I was imagining things, until she followed me across seven rows at the supermarket, videoing me with her phone.

This too will pass, right? I know that pretty much all news is temporary. Scandals are like waves that crash on the beach, then quietly retreat in foam, but when it's about you, it seems like there is no other news. It feels like every spotlight is on you as the public watches from the gallery like voyeurs, their faces darkened and entertained by the drama of your life.

Obviously, I've thought this over too much. The thing is, I couldn't stop thinking about it. I'm just compulsive enough that I suppose I would have continued down my crazy spiral until I self-destructed or until something else unexpected turned up. Fortunately, it did. Actually, someone. A stranger. And he came at Christmas.

CHAPTER
Two

Was I a fool to trust him? I suppose the last people to think themselves fools are fools.

—Maggie Walther's Diary

WEDNESDAY, NOVEMBER 9

The story of my stranger began on a subfreezing November morning, the aftermath of a series of local blizzards. I was sitting alone near the window of the Grounds for Coffee. Not surprisingly, the coffee shop wasn't as busy as usual. The latest blizzard had dropped a blanket over the city, and the usual traffic warning went out: Don't leave the house unless necessary. I had no idea why Carina, my business assistant and best friend—my only friend—had been so insistent at meeting at the coffee shop this morning. She wouldn't take no for an answer, even though I'd said it at least four times. I hadn't left my house for nearly a week. I looked like it. No makeup. My unwashed, unbrushed hair was mostly concealed beneath a baseball cap.

The shop had its usual blend of clientele—as eclectic and caffeinated as their concoctions. I

13

was the only one sitting alone, so I leafed through the newspaper to hide my awkwardness. I turned to the local section of the paper only to see a haggard-looking mug shot of Clive. It seemed that every time there was a discussion about the mayoral race or a vote of the city council, Clive's picture would be dragged up. The article du jour was about the woman the mayor had nominated to fill my husband's position.

Honestly, I couldn't tell you what's worse—the betrayal, the public humiliation, or the question that was on everyone's mind: *"How did you not know that your husband had another family?"*

They just didn't understand. Some people have husbands who come home from work, grab a beer, and watch TV all night. These people are not married to a politician or anyone in the public spotlight. Every night there's an event, an Elks club gathering or a women's political caucus. If I hadn't put my foot down, he'd have been gone every night and weekend.

Or maybe I really was just as dumb as everyone thought.

I knew he was cheating on me; I just thought it was with his career. Politics had always been his second wife. I mean, he didn't even have time for me. How could he possibly have time for another wife and family?

Looking back, I realized there were clues. My last birthday he gave me a leather miniskirt.

When I looked surprised, he said, "But that's what you asked for." It wasn't something I had or ever would have asked for.

Another time, before going to bed, he called me Jen, which, incidentally, is half the name of the other woman. Jennifer. It is also the name of one of the other council members, so it was easy for him to explain it away, and for me to brush it off. I just chalked it all up to his overtaxed brain and schedule. I wish I had been more suspicious. But then, there's a lot of things I wish I had done differently.

CHAPTER
Three

Carina thinks I need to change my environment to something more cheerful, like switching the song on the radio. To me it feels more like putting an ice cube in the microwave.

—Maggie Walther's Diary

Carina walked into the coffee shop about fifteen minutes late, escorted by a flurry of snow. She wore red leather gloves, a thick parka, and a red wool scarf with a matching beret strategically placed over her perfectly trimmed blond hair. She always dressed as if everyone was looking at her, and I suppose they were, probably *because* she dressed like everyone was looking at her. And she was pretty. Although she was seven years younger than me, people often said we looked alike, or asked if we were sisters. I doubt anyone would now. The contrast between our grooming made me feel self-conscious.

She looked around the room until she found me, then walked over, unpeeling her scarf as she walked. "Hi, love. Sorry I'm late. The roads were horrific." She leaned over and kissed me on the cheek. "I passed three accidents and at least a dozen cars off the road."

"I was almost one of them," I said.

"That's because my washing machine's bigger than your Fiat."

"No, that's *because* we should have stayed home."

"No," she said, unzipping her coat. "More time at home is the last thing you need right now." She sat down. "That's why I wanted to meet here. To get you out of your black hole of misery."

"Into the blinding bright world of misery?" I lifted the newspaper to show her Clive's picture.

"He looks wretched," she said. She looked me over. "Speaking of which, how much weight have you lost?"

"Nice segue."

"You look like a waif. You need to eat more. And you need to get out."

I collapsed back into my chair. "I'm too tired to get out."

"That's depression, honey. And you'll stay that way until you get out."

"I don't want to get out. I'm a pariah."

Carina touched her coffee cup. "I don't even know what that means."

"It means I'm an untouchable. A social leper."

Carina shook her head. "No, you're not."

"No one wants to be seen with me."

"I do."

"Besides you," I said. "And you're a poor judge of character."

"I am not."

I cocked my head to one side.

"Maybe in dating," she relented. "And marriage." Carina had been married twice, once to a man who had been married seven times before, the other to a guy who just left one day and never came back. She found out later that he was wanted for check fraud in eleven states. "You know what you need?"

"Cyanide pills?"

Carina frowned. "You need to get involved with something outside yourself. Like come back to work."

"I'm sorry," I said. "I'm not ready for that yet."

"Then at least change your environment. I drove by your house the other night and all the lights were out. It was only eight."

"You should have just rung the doorbell."

"I did." She raised three fingers. "Three times."

"I was sleeping. I've been sleeping weird hours lately. It's like my body doesn't know the difference between day and night. Did you know that during the winter months, beavers stay inside their lodges almost all the time? And since there are no light cues—like day or night—they develop their own circadian rhythm of twenty-nine-hour days."

Carina stared at me for a moment, then said, "I don't know if I'm more disturbed that you know this or that you're telling me this." Her eyes narrowed. "Why are you telling me this?"

"I saw it on a documentary . . ."

"While you were holed up in your lodge," she said.

"Yes, while I was holed up in my lodge. And I'm telling you this because it resonated with me. My circadian rhythm is off. I get up in the middle of the night and can't sleep."

Her gaze intensified. "You're isolating. And identifying with beavers."

I frowned. "I know."

"Well, if you're not going to leave your home, at least bring some life into it."

"You want me to invite some other woodland creatures to join me?"

She grinned. "What I mean is that you need to shake things up. Right after my first divorce I read a book on breakups, and it suggested changing around your physical environment to help change your emotional environment. It was by Benjamin Hardy. It worked for me. Clean the house, buy new furniture, decorate. It's Christmas, put some lights up or something. Do you even have a Christmas tree?"

"Having a tree would mean the holidays are coming."

"The holidays *are* coming. Get a tree."

I took a sip of my coffee. "That's not going to happen."

"Why not?"

"To begin with, I don't feel *Christmasy*."

"Is that even a word?"

"It is now."

"Well, you don't feel *Christmasy* because you're not acting *Christmasy*. It's a verb, not a noun."

"Actually, it's an adjective."

"Don't get grammatical on me. Bottom line, you're alone. And loneliness is dangerous. Studies have shown it's more hazardous to your health than smoking or being overweight. Especially during the holidays. There's a reason so many people commit suicide during the holidays."

"That's a myth," I said. "The suicide rate is highest in spring. It always has been."

She eyed me suspiciously. "How did you know that?"

"I'm not considering suicide, if that's what you're thinking." She continued to look at me doubtfully and I threw one hand up. "You brought it up, not me."

Carina was quiet. After a moment she said, "Do you know the first thing you're supposed to do if you're lost in the woods?"

I looked at her blankly. "And you're mocking me about the beaver lodge?"

"There's a point to this."

"I'm dying to see where you're going with this."

"First thing you do, you build a fire. Do you know why?"

"To keep warm."

"No, to keep busy. To keep your mind from panicking. That's what you need."

"You think I should set fire to Clive's car?"

"That's what I'm talking about, Mag. No matter the conversation, you bring it back to him like a magnet. You've got to get out of that. It's not about him, it's about you. You need to reclaim your life." Her voice softened. "Look, I understand why you want to isolate. I really do. But it's not the answer. You need to show Clive that he can't take away your life."

"He did take away my life."

"No, he took away your situation. You're still here. Life isn't through with you. You never know what's around the corner."

"That's what I'm afraid of."

She reached over and put her hand on mine. "This will pass, love. It's okay that you're lying low for now. No one can blame you for that. I just don't want to see this crush your spirit."

I looked down for a moment, then back up into Carina's sympathetic eyes. Tears suddenly filled my own, as the words I'd been thinking for weeks spilled out. "Why wasn't I enough for him?"

"No one could be enough for him," Carina said, sliding her chair closer. "Some people just have holes they can't fill. That's hard for you to understand because you're not that way. Clive was insatiable. He always wanted more. That's why he was always running for something bigger. He wanted more people to love him. He didn't understand that one person's love is better than a thousand people's approval."

I started crying more, and she put her arms around me. "Oh, honey. This will pass."

When I could speak I said, "Are you sure?"

"It will pass if you let it," she said. "Think about what I said about changing things up. I think it will help." She looked into my eyes. "Will you?"

I nodded.

She smiled. "Good girl. Now when are you coming back to work?"

CHAPTER
Four

Sometimes our past follows us like toilet paper stuck to the heel of our shoe as we walk out of the bathroom. And we're always the last one to see it.

—Maggie Walther's Diary

I didn't have an answer for her question. I felt guilty leaving Carina alone during the busiest time of the year. Ironically, it's the exact same thing that had happened to me just before my company's previous owner passed the business on to me.

But my absence from work was more than just isolation. It was confusion. The catering business, my broken childhood, and Clive were all complexly tied together in a knot. I felt like I was trying to find my way through a confusing labyrinth that just kept taking me back to where I had started.

Where I had started. I was born and raised in Ashland, Oregon, just sixteen miles north of the California border. It's a peculiar place. Today it's extremely liberal—so much so that some of the neighboring communities refer to it as "the People's Republic of Ashland." They'd probably like to forget that their city fathers once held Klan parades downtown and advertised themselves as a haven for "American citizens—negroes and Japanese not welcome."

But times change and so do people and locales. The scenery is beautiful there, mostly woods and mountains. Sounds like an idyllic place for a little boy and girl to grow up. My childhood should have been idyllic, but it wasn't. My childhood was ugly.

If I had to sum up the reason for my pain in one word, I'd say, "My father." (Okay, two words.) My father never should have had children. Of course that means my brother and I wouldn't have been born, but sometimes I'm not sure that would have been such a bad thing.

My father never should have even gotten married. I don't know why he did. He was always cheating on my mother. I couldn't tell you how many times he cheated because I don't know if he ever wasn't. Sometimes there were fights; most of the time I just saw the pain and resignation on my mother's face. I could never understand why my mother didn't just leave. Eventually she did, just not the way I thought she would.

The end of their union came during my fourteenth year. My mother went in to one of those surgical centers for a routine colonoscopy. She developed complications and died. I still remember the look on the doctor's face when he told us. I didn't believe it until I saw her breathless body. I remember feeling angry at her for not taking me with her.

I've learned that everyone handles grief differently. My brother, Eric, just disappeared, first within himself, then, years later, physically. I don't know how my father handled the loss of his wife; the only emotion he ever shared was anger. I suspect that, among other things, he felt guilt. Maybe I just hope that he did, like a real human would. But I think he also recognized the opportunity—not that my mother kept him away from other women—but her presence kept other women away. At least the kind with a scrap of dignity. I could never figure out why my father wanted women so badly, then treated them so badly.

As far as our home life, my father pretty much just checked out. Six months after my mother's death, my father sued the doctor and clinic for malpractice and got all sorts of money. He bought himself a really big boat, the kind that could cross the ocean. I still had to beg him for grocery money.

I wanted to go to college, but I knew my father wouldn't pay for it. I asked him about it once and he said college was indoctrination, not education, and that he had already taught me all I needed to know about the world.

I learned young that whatever I wanted in life,

I would have to get for myself. Fortunately, or unfortunately, I developed young, so I always looked older than I was. Everyone assumed I was twenty when I was barely fifteen. My first job was as a server at a local café. Every day old men hit on me. Looking back, I suppose they weren't really that old, probably in their thirties and forties, but they seemed ancient to me.

When I was a senior in high school, Eric ran away. He left me a note that read, "Good-bye, I'm sorry." That was it. No address, nothing. I didn't need to ask why. It was the same reason that I wanted to leave home, except my father was even worse to him than he was to me. It seemed to me that with Eric, my father was constantly trying to prove that he was the alpha dog.

Two weeks after I graduated from high school, I moved to Utah. It wasn't the kind of place I thought I'd end up. In fact, up until six months before moving there, I knew nothing about the place. It was just one of those peculiar twists of fate that pulls the seat out from under you.

One day I was talking to one of the truckers at the café—we had tons of them—who was hauling a load of lumber to his hometown of Salt Lake City. I asked him what Salt Lake City was like. He said he liked it. It was bigger than Ashland, smaller than Portland. He said there was the University of Utah, which would be cheap once I got residence, and in the meantime there was a lot of work there. The cost of living was low and the people pretty much left you alone, except the Mormons, who would probably bring me a loaf of home-baked bread and invite me to church. Best of all, it was seven hundred miles from my father.

With Eric gone, I didn't really have anything holding me in Ashland. I had a cute boyfriend, Carter, but I wasn't in love or anything, and even though he talked about marriage (which I always thought was a little bizarre for an eighteen-year-old), I knew he wasn't someone I wanted to spend the rest of my life with.

I wasn't afraid to leave home. After what I'd been through, I don't think I was afraid of much. I was, by necessity, frugal, so between my waitressing and tips and the occasional babysitting, I'd saved about five thousand dollars, which my father never knew about. Even with all his money, I have no doubt that he would have cleaned me out if he did, then justify his action as another one of his life lessons.

About a month before graduation, I started looking around for someplace to live in Utah. I came across a want ad posted by a young woman looking for a roommate. Her name was Wendy Nielsen. She had just quit her job working for a catering company and even though her rent was only three hundred and seventy-five dollars a month, she couldn't afford it.

The place looked nice online. Then I asked her about work. I had some cooking experience at the restaurant and had done almost all the cooking at home, so I asked if there was an opening at the catering company she'd just left.

"There's always an opening," she replied. "The owner's a witch. She runs everyone off. She's like barely five-foot and she has a massive mole on her left cheek. Her name is Marge."

I hesitated a moment, then said, "She named her mole Marge?"

Wendy laughed so hard she had to run to the bathroom. We were friends before we even met.

Wendy was right about the catering job. They were hiring. Perpetually. Not only were the wages good—$18.50 an hour, which was more than double what I'd ever made before—but I also got tips. Sometimes big ones. And there were insurance benefits.

"It's not worth a hundred dollars an hour," Wendy told me. "It's psychological abuse. You'll end up paying more for a good therapist."

"Do they have mental health benefits?" I asked.

The thing was, I wasn't really afraid of anyone, and I needed better money than I was going to make waitressing. I figured I could do anything for a year. Catering certainly wasn't something I had planned on making a career.

Actually, at that point I had no idea what I was going to do with my life, as I had been more focused on what I didn't want it to be than what I wanted it to be. The job was just something I could do while I made up my mind.

It was also perfect timing for me, since I couldn't go to school until I had established residency and could apply for a grant. I was one of those kids in a bind: my father had too much money for me to get student aid, but he wasn't willing to give me any of it. I was stuck.

Wendy had understated the pay but not her former employer. Marge Watson burned through employees like cars burn through tires at the Indianapolis 500. She was professional enough to never scold an employee in front of a client, but that was about the extent of her self-discipline. She'd eat employees for breakfast. She was good at it, and since most of her employees were young kids who had never worked before, they never lasted long.

Her personality didn't faze me. Compared to my father, she was a kitten. And unlike my father, she couldn't hit me—though Wendy told me that she did slap an employee once. The employee sued, and the slap ended up costing Marge thousands of dollars. She never hit anyone after that.

Still, I knew it was only a matter of time before she came after me, so I waited for my turn, not with fear but with curiosity. I wondered what I would do.

Outside of me and the revolving door of part-time employees, there were two Mexican women who also worked full time: Frida and Eiza. Marge wasn't nice to them either, but they never seemed to mind her rants. I wasn't sure if it was a cultural thing, if they needed the money too much, or if they just didn't really understand what she was saying, as neither of them spoke English very well.

Finally my day came. I had a confrontation with a trust-fund bridezilla who had had too much to drink and suddenly insisted that she had ordered a four-tier wedding cake instead of a three. I wasn't sure if she thought I was going to quickly bake her a new tier or what her endgame was, but I just brushed her off.

Then she shoved me. She shouldn't have done that. I threw her up against a wall and, with my forearm across her throat, said, "You touch me again and your wedding pictures will look like something out of a Stephen King movie."

When I let her go, she ran out crying. Of course the bride's mother went ballistic on Marge, who of course then came after me. Marge was blue in the face and yelled at me until I thought she might burst a blood vessel. I just looked at her, unaffected. I think she thought I would quit, like everyone else did, but I was going to make her fire me so I could collect unemployment if I had to.

Neither happened. When she finished her tirade,

I said calmly, "You should try Prozac. And breath mints." Then I walked out the back door.

As I was about to get into my car, Marge poked her head out the door and shouted to me, "I am on Prozac. Don't be late Monday."

Marge never got mad at me after that. I was probably the first employee who had ever stood up to her and, in so doing, had earned her respect. It was almost like she was testing me—like at the end of the first Willy Wonka movie. The good one.

When I started, Just Desserts only did weddings and an occasional bar mitzvah. (Utah, due to its religious culture, has a myriad of the former and a dearth of the latter.) Then people began asking us to do their company parties and corporate catering. As we expanded, Marge taught me everything she knew about the trade.

After that first year, Marge offered me a sizable raise to delay college and work full time for the company. I'm not really sure why Marge started the company to begin with, other than she was fiercely independent and didn't like the idea of living in her husband's shadow. Her husband, Craig, was the CEO of a local plumbing supply company. I only met him a few times, but he was a good-looking, clean-cut man, always perfectly coiffed. One of those shiny people like Clive. He and Marge were about as compatible as mayonnaise and maple syrup.

I have no idea what brought the two of them together. He was soft-spoken, kind, and respectful, and Marge was Marge. She treated him like dirt. I always felt sorry for him.

Peculiarly, I had worked for Marge for more than a year before I found out she had a daughter. Tabitha. Not surprisingly, they didn't get along. From what I gathered, Tabitha wanted to be a playwright and lived, with a credit card from her father, in New York City, working backstage on off-Broadway productions.

As time passed, I realized that I was Marge's only friend. I also sensed that she was getting bored with the business, as she gave me more and more responsibility until I was pretty much running the place. (Kind of like what I was presently doing with Carina.) After two more years Marge doubled my salary and made me the chief operating officer, which meant I still did the same thing, I just got paid for it.

Then, one snowy February morning, Marge called me as I was getting ready for work. Her voice was hoarse and a little stiffer than usual.

"Craig's gone," she said.

"Gone where?" I asked.

"He had a heart attack while he was shoveling the walk. He's gone."

She was so stoic that I wasn't sure how to respond. "I'm sorry."

"I won't be coming in," she said.

I didn't see her for almost nine weeks. Then, two weeks after my twenty-third birthday, Marge asked to meet me for lunch at her favorite restaurant, a local bistro run by German people who were as rude as she was.

I got to the restaurant a few minutes early. Marge still hadn't arrived, so the hostess sat me and brought me a drink. Ten minutes later Marge walked in. I almost didn't recognize her. I couldn't believe how much she had changed in just a short time. She'd already been skinny, but now she looked gaunt, her skin tight on her cheeks, which made her look old. Her hair had turned completely gray. I don't know if the stress of her husband's death had gotten to her or if she had just stopped coloring it. Maybe both.

"Have you ordered yet?" she asked, sitting down. I thought it was a strange thing to say to someone you hadn't seen in over two months.

"No. I was waiting for you."

"Who's your waitress?"

I pointed to a young, flaxen-haired woman setting drinks at another table. "Her."

"You," Marge shouted to the young woman. "We're ready to order now."

"I'll be right there," the waitress said, looking somewhere between annoyed and stunned. A moment later she walked over. "Are you ready to order?"

"I just told you we were," Marge said. "Now

get out your little notepad there. We'll have the red hummus appetizer to share, then I'll have a bowl of the sweet potato soup, and tell the chef that if he puts too much turmeric in it this time, I'll make him eat it."

The server let out a short sigh, wrote down the order, then turned to me. "What can I get for you?"

"*May,*" Marge interrupted. "What *may* I get for you. You're a professional, honey. If you're going to work with the public, you need to speak their language."

The woman flushed. By then I was not surprised by Marge's utter lack of social finesse, but I still felt bad for the young woman.

"What may I get for you?" she asked, noticeably softer.

"I'll have a spring salad, with the dressing on the side," I said. "Thank you."

She gathered our menus. "All right, I'll be right back with your appetizer."

After she was gone, Marge said, "I'm sorry I missed your birthday." That was one of the surprise quirks of Marge's personality. She kept track of all her employees' birthdays and, no matter how tenuous their employment, would commemorate them by coming in early to bake one of her raspberry almond cakes.

"It's okay. You've had a lot on your plate," I said.

She sighed deeply. "I didn't realize how heavy the grief would be." She seemed annoyed by this, as if her husband's death had been more of an inconvenience than she expected. "I've felt crazy."

"I thought the same thing when my mother died."

"I have a present for you." She reached into her purse and brought out an envelope, which she handed to me. I hoped there was money inside. There wasn't. There was only a birthday card with one of our business cards with my name on it. All the card said was *Happy Birthday.*

I didn't really understand why she was giving me one of my own business cards.

"Thank you," I said.

"You didn't read the card," she said.

"I read it."

"I meant the business card. Read it."

I looked back down and saw *Just Desserts. Maggie Walther. Owner.*

Owner. I looked up at her.

"I don't want to do this anymore," she said.

Her comment was a little odd since she really hadn't done anything with the business for months. "Do what?"

"The business. It's time I retired. I hate our clients and I have no desire to spend the rest of my life freezing my bones in Utah. I'm moving to Sun City, Arizona." I didn't know there was such a place but it sounded nice. "There's no one else who could run my business."

"What about Tabitha?"

"Oh, please."

"You could sell it," I said.

"To who? Some moron who would run it into the ground after I've put my best years into it? And then I'd have her calling me every time she had a problem. You know I don't need the money. Craig left me with more than I can spend. Besides, you're more a daughter than my own daughter."

It was the sweetest thing she had ever said to me. Maybe to anyone. "Thank you."

"You're the only thing that has made the last few years remotely tolerable."

"Thank you," I said again. "I'll miss you."

She said, "Yeah. Don't get sentimental on me. You know I hate that crap."

The waitress returned carrying our meals. She pretty much dropped the food on the table and ran. I watched in anticipation as Marge tried her soup. She took a second spoonful, so I knew we were safe. "When are you leaving?" I asked.

"I put the house up for sale last Monday. It's already under contract."

"You mean the kitchen?" I asked. Our company headquarters was an old home that Marge had converted into a commercial kitchen and bakery. She usually just called it "the house."

"No, not the kitchen. You're going to need that. I meant my personal residence."

"That's fast," I said. "That's good."

"It means I sold too cheap." She shook her head. "What's done is done. The buyers want to close by April third, so I'm flying to Arizona tomorrow to find a place. I'll have Scott finish up the paperwork so we can legally transfer the company over before I leave. We'll need to transfer all the bank accounts into your name. I'll leave a cushion in there, but I doubt you'll need it. We have six thousand in receivables. There's at least fifty grand in equity on the kitchen."

"I'll pay you back when I can," I said.

"I don't want you paying me back. It's a signing bonus. We already have more than a hundred thousand in contracts. You'll do okay."

"I don't know what to say."

"Just eat your salad," she said.

I saw Marge only once after that. She died of cancer just eighteen weeks later. I found out later that she'd had stage four uterine cancer when she had turned over the business. She never even told me. She hated pity. There were only three of us at her funeral. Tabitha didn't even come.

CHAPTER
Five

An anonymous woman posted her sympathy online for me, saying that she too
had been "Clived." In spite of my pain, I
almost laughed. You never want to live to
see your name become a verb.
—Maggie Walther's Diary

I met Clive six months before I took over the
company while we were catering a political soiree
for the Salt Lake mayor's race. The event was
held at the National Society of the Sons of Utah
Pioneers convention hall. The room was filled
with suits and pantsuits—ambitious political
types. Clive was there, younger than most, yet
swimming through the crowd as effortlessly as
a koi in a backyard pond. He was already in his
second year of law school and was clerking at the
firm he would eventually become a partner at.

I thought he was handsome, though not in
a way I was used to. Most of the guys I dated
had long hair and tattoos. Clive looked perfectly
arranged, from his flawlessly knotted tie to his
expensive-looking shoes. His hair looked better
cared for than mine. From my experience, those

kinds of guys might give you a second look but never a second date. We shared eye contact as I came from the kitchen carrying a tray of hors d'oeuvres to the room.

He immediately took a step toward me. "I'll have one of those," he said, lifting a bacon-wrapped chestnut from my tray.

I might have been flirting. I don't remember. "Just one?"

"Let me see." He popped the morsel into his mouth, ate it, then took another. "Did you make these?"

"No."

"You just serve the food."

"No. I bake. I just made other things."

"What do you think of this party?"

"I'm working," I said.

"We all are," he replied. "The laughter is fake. Bunch of sycophants. Are you partisan?"

"No," I said. "I'm Pisces."

He burst out laughing. "That's the best thing I've heard all night. I'm a Leo. King of the jungle."

"Which jungle?"

"Whichever one will run when I roar," he said, a slight smile bending his mouth. "Pisces and Leo. We're compatible opposites."

"I need to get back to work," I said.

"What time do you get off work?"

"Long after the party is over."

"Is that a brush-off?"

"No. It's a fact."

"May I have your phone number?"

"You don't even know my name."

"That would be helpful," he said. "What's your name?"

"Maggie. What's yours?"

"Clive. Like Clive Davis."

"Your last name is Davis?"

"No. Clive Davis is a famous record producer."

"Never heard of him," I said.

"He signed the greats. Janis Joplin, Aerosmith, Billy Joel, Bruce Springsteen, the Grateful Dead."

"All before my time, but yes."

"Yes, you've heard of them?"

"Yes, you can have my phone number."

He pulled out his phone. "Go ahead."

"It's 555-2412."

"That's not a fake number, is it?"

"Do women often give you fake numbers?" He didn't answer. "If I didn't want you to call me, I'd tell you."

"That's refreshing," he said. He typed something into his phone. "I just texted you." I guessed he was testing me, waiting to see if something on me would buzz or ding. "Nothing."

"I'm not allowed to have my phone on while I work."

"That makes sense."

"I'm also not supposed to mingle with the guests. I've got to get back to work."

"I'll call you tomorrow."

"I hope you do."

He smiled and walked away, disappearing back into the crowd. I replenished the table. When I got back to the kitchen, Marge said, "Who was that man you were talking to?"

"No one."

"But you gave him your phone number."

"Yes."

"This is the last place I'd give anyone a phone number."

I should have listened to her. Clive called me early the next morning. I was still in bed. We hadn't left the party until midnight, and I hadn't gotten to bed until half past one.

"Hello," I said groggily.

"Rise and shine, princess," he said.

I rubbed my eyes. "Who is this?"

"Clive, from the party last night. May I take you to breakfast?"

"What time is it?"

"Seven."

"I was asleep. Who calls at seven?"

"Apparently I do. I couldn't get you off my mind."

"I don't know if I should be flattered or scared."

"I think you need more sleep," he said. "Tell you what, why don't I pick you up at noon and

41

I'll take you to La Caille for brunch." La Caille
was an expensive French restaurant tucked away
in the canyons.

"Okay," I said.

"I'll see you then."

"Wait. You don't know where I live."

"Actually, I do. I'll see you at noon."

He hung up the phone.

How does he know where I live? I was too tired
to think. I rolled over and went back to sleep.

Clive showed up on time. I had brunch with
him, then dinner, then breakfast. We dated for
only two months before he asked me to marry
him. I said yes.

CHAPTER
Six

Some days it's just best not to leave the bunker.

—Maggie Walther's Diary

On the drive home I thought about what Carina had said—at least when I wasn't worrying about sliding off the road and dying in a car accident. She was right. I knew that I needed to do something to get out of my funk. Or at least my bedroom. An undeniable part of me longed for normalcy. The idea of changing my environment and embracing Christmas made sense. The thing was, I loved Christmas. I always had.

This was one place where Clive and I were in sync. Clive was also big on Christmas. (Why can't I say *big* without thinking *bigamy?*) Typical Clive, he went overboard. Our house wasn't just dressed for the season, it was custom-decorated by the local commercial display company. I knew it had gotten too extreme when people began stopping in front of our house to take pictures. Our electric bill tripled during the season.

Every year got worse, and I fully expected our home to someday evolve into a Macy's-like

Christmas attraction with window displays and long lines of spectators and pretzel carts.

All this attention to the season wasn't really for us. It was for Clive's schmoozers—my word, not his—who came to our parties. Clive was big on parties and he kept long lists of attendees, each carefully arranged and cross-checked against each other to keep the wrong people from attending the same party. He even invited his enemies to our parties, following the admonition to keep your friends close but your enemies closer.

With the exception of the other attorneys' wives, whom I superficially knew, I didn't know any of the people at the parties. Our home was basically another catering job, except I was also the hostess, smiling prettily as I told people where the bathrooms were, took their coats, and put coasters under their drinks.

In a moment of weakness, I had imagined what Clive's other wife's home looked like at Christmas. The thought of it made my stomach hurt.

When I got home, my front walk and driveway, like the rest of the world, were covered with snow. I pulled into my garage, grabbed a snow shovel, and spent the next hour shoveling the driveway and sidewalk until my back hurt.

As I was finishing up, it started to snow again. First in wispy, pretty flakes, then increasing in density until the sky seemed to be more snow than not. Within minutes the concrete I'd cleared was covered again. Defeated, I went back inside the house and curled up in bed. This was not a day to be out. The world had it in for me.

CHAPTER
Seven

The storm just keeps on coming—literally and figuratively.
—Maggie Walther's Diary

The storm got worse. Wondering if the world had slipped into an ice age that I hadn't been warned about, I actually turned on the local news. I say "actually" because it was the first time in a long time. For obvious reasons I had been avoiding the news, but I really wanted to see what they had to say about the weather. According to the annoyingly spunky weatherwoman, the storm wasn't slackening anytime soon. Worst case, it was supposed to shut down the city. I didn't really care. At least it made my isolation excusable.

After the news, I watched some show about a crazy woman who had killed her husband, then tried to dispose of the body by feeding it to her neighbor's pigs. That's the kind of mood I was in.

Around ten o'clock the power went out. I used my cell phone as a flashlight to walk around the house. I found some candles, which I lit in the kitchen. I hadn't eaten anything all day and I was feeling it. I made myself a turkey and cheddar cheese sandwich, which even by candlelight wasn't romantic in the least.

Then I just lay on the couch waiting for the lights to come back on. They didn't. After an hour the power was still out and though the house was warmed by natural gas, the heater's controls ran on electronics, so the house kept getting colder.

I raised a blind to look outside. Even though it was nearly midnight, it was eerily light out, as the blizzardscape was illuminated by a full moon. The snow on the ground was already at least two feet deep.

I began to worry about the cold. One of the problems with isolation is that your imagination begins to create its own reality. I pictured myself being the subject of one of those stories the papers always run after a major storm, where a home's heat was shut off and the occupant is found, days later, frozen to death.

In the basement, we had an antique-looking wood-burning stove that we rarely used. Actually, never used. It had come with the house, and we had thought of it only as decoration: the polished copper firewood tub next to it had never been emptied of carefully stacked logs. Briefly, I wondered if the logs were still good or if they'd expired, which might have been the dumbest thing I'd ever thought—with the exception of believing that my husband loved only me.

I struggled with starting the fire for more than

twenty minutes before shouting out, "I hate being alone!" I'm not entirely sure what being alone had to do with starting a fire, but my loneliness suddenly felt as heavy and cold as the air around me. I realized something. Marriage had changed me. I had once insisted on my alone time. Now I feared it.

As for the fire, I finally just filled the whole stove with newspapers, covered them with wood, then doused the whole thing in some lighter fluid I found in the garage. (Clive prided himself on being a barbecue "purist" and used one of those old charcoal-burning, wire-grilled barbecues.) The stove almost exploded, but the fire was going.

I got my pillow and a quilt from upstairs, then lay down on the couch in front of the crackling fire. As I watched the flickering flames, I remembered what Carina had said at the coffee shop about starting a fire when you're lost in the wilderness. I was lost in an emotional wilderness, and I needed all the help I could get.

CHAPTER
Eight

Why do I still miss him? Or is it just the myth of him that I miss? How much of each relationship is based on reality versus what we hope to believe about who the other person is?

—Maggie Walther's Diary

I woke sometime around three in the morning when the power came back on and the lights and television with it. I hadn't bothered to turn the lights on downstairs, so the room was lit only by the lamp in the stairwell and the glowing orange embers in the stove.

I went upstairs, blew out the candles, then turned off all the lights and the television. I checked the thermostat. The temperature had fallen to sixty-three degrees but the furnace had finally kicked on. I climbed in between the cold sheets of my bed and closed my eyes. As angry and betrayed as I felt about Clive, I missed him next to me—the warmth of his body, the soothing sound of his breathing. Three questions bounced around inside my skull, each taking its turn to inflict its pain like tag team wrestlers: *Why did he betray me? What's wrong with me? Why wasn't I enough?*

CHAPTER
Nine

Lynch mobs never went away. They just migrated to the Internet.
—Maggie Walther's Diary

That night I had a peculiar dream. I was following Clive, barefoot, through a snowy forest. I asked him where we were going. "Nowhere," he replied. "Then why are we walking?" I asked. He turned around. He was wearing a mask. I asked him to take it off. He said, "Are you sure?" I said yes. He lifted the mask. There was nothing there.

I woke, my heart pounding fiercely. The sun was projecting its bright rays through the partially open wooden slats of my window blinds. I could hear the neighborhood snowblower brigade, their machines' engines whining and chugging beneath the weight of the night's snow. A reminder that outside my shuttered world, life was carrying on as usual.

My body ached nearly as much as my heart. I forced myself out of bed and walked over and lifted the blinds. The light was intense, the morning sun reflecting off the newly laid crystalline blanket. The sky was bright blue and the storm was gone, but it had left behind nearly thirty inches. My neighbor's Volkswagen, which had been parked in the street, looked more like an igloo than a car.

Now I really was snowed in and my back still ached from the few inches of snow I'd shoveled the night before. I didn't want to go out in public, but I needed to. I needed to prove to myself that the world wasn't laughing at me. I know that sounds paranoid, but there's a reason. After Clive's story broke, I made the mistake of reading the comments people posted online about the newspaper story. Many of them were directed at me, some mocking me, some blaming me. I was astounded to see such viciousness from people I didn't know and who didn't know me.

I once read that people, when cloaked in anonymity, would do things they wouldn't otherwise do—hence the invention of the masquerade party. When did society get so mean?

CHAPTER
Ten

Sometimes the simplicity of a kind act is inversely proportionate to the power of its effect.
> —Maggie Walther's Diary

I walked to my front door to see just how snowed in I was. As I opened the door, the freezing air on my face felt bracing. In the bright light, it took me a moment to understand what I was seeing. Someone had plowed my driveway, sidewalk, and walkway. On my doorstep was a red glass candle with a note taped to it. I stooped to pick it up.

> Dear Maggie,
> My husband and I wanted you to know how sorry we are for what you are going through. You're in our prayers. Please let us know if there's anything we can do.
>> Sincerely,
>> Bryan and Leisa Stephens

Even though I'd lived across the street from them for more than three years, I hardly knew them. I saw them out walking their dog now and then—a miniature Maltese poodle—but our interactions had been scarcely more than a wave.

I looked across the street at their house. It looked dark. I wanted to show them my appreciation, so I decided to do what I did best. Bake. One of my most popular Christmas confections was thumbprint cookies—small, silver dollar–sized sugar cookies. I would press each with my thumb, then fill the indentation with a spoonful of jam.

I decided I should at least make myself presentable enough to not scare them. I showered, put on makeup, and did my hair. For the first time in weeks, I looked human again.

I went out to the kitchen and preset the oven, then started mixing ingredients. Thumbprint cookies are easy to make, a simple recipe of flour, baking powder, butter, sugar, eggs, and vanilla. Simple or not, I found myself enjoying the feeling of being absorbed in something other than my problems.

I scooped out balls of dough with a small ice cream scoop and pressed my thumb into each ball, flattening it and leaving an indentation, before adding the jam. After they baked, I filled a plate with the cookies, covered it with plastic wrap, and wrote a short note:

Dear Bryan and Leisa,
Thank you for your thoughtfulness during

this difficult time. It means more than you know.

Sincerely,
Maggie

I put my coat back on, walked across the street to their home, and pushed the doorbell. A moment later I heard footsteps, then the door unlocked. A dowdy middle-aged woman in a jumpsuit answered. "May I help you?"

Even though she didn't look familiar, I didn't know the Stephenses well enough to know if the woman was Leisa or not. I assumed she was. "Hi. I wanted to thank you for what you and your husband did for me this morning."

"I think you're mistaking me for my sister," she said.

"I'm sorry. Is Leisa or Bryan home?"

"They left half an hour ago."

The exchange felt awkward.

"Well, I brought them some cookies." I offered the plate. "They're still warm. I just wanted to say thank you. Bryan shoveled my driveway and walk."

"He would do that." She took the plate from me without looking at it.

"Do you expect them back soon?"

"Not until Thursday. They're going to be up in Logan a few days." Then, after a pause, she added, "Their son was killed yesterday in a snowmobiling accident."

The pronouncement stunned me. "I'm so sorry."

"It's a tragedy. He has four children, and his wife already suffers from depression."

I didn't know what to say. Finally, I said again, "I'm sorry."

"Who should I say came by?"

"I'm Maggie Walther," I said. "My name's on the note. I'll reach out next week."

She thanked me vicariously for the Stephenses and shut the door. I turned and walked back to my house. I was moved by the couple's circumstance. As appreciative as I had already been for their kindness, now I was astounded. In the midst of such heartbreak, this good couple had reached out to me in my pain. For the first time in a long while, I felt hope in humanity.

CHAPTER
Eleven

I went to find a Christmas tree. I found something else.

— Maggie Walther's Diary

When I got home, I walked around the house opening the blinds, then turned on the radio. Not surprisingly, it was set to one of the local talk stations. I immediately started pushing other presets, stopping at a station playing Christmas music.

Christmas music has always been healing to me. I thought again of my good neighbors and their ability to transcend their grief. You don't find light looking in the dark, and consciously or not, for the last six months I had resigned myself to the dark, scurrying from light like a cockroach. I was ready to at least try to lift myself out of it. Maybe lifting the blinds had been a literal manifestation of that.

Burl Ives sang "Have a Holly, Jolly Christmas." I smiled, which was another groundbreaking achievement. When was the last time I'd smiled? Carina was right, I needed to change my environment. What would be more fitting than a Christmas tree?

I finished cleaning my kitchen, put on my long wool coat, and went out to my car. I drove to the Kroger's where I'd noticed a Christmas tree lot on the south corner of their parking lot.

In Salt Lake, like in most big cities, Christmas tree lots started springing up around November— usually in the corner of a mall or supermarket's parking lot. I remembered, as a girl, a place in Ashland where one of the Christmas tree lots had a fenced-in corral of Santa's reindeer. It was one of the few truly magical memories that had somehow survived the trauma of my childhood.

The traffic was light; it took me less than ten minutes to reach my destination. The Christmas tree lot was about a half-acre square and surrounded by a portable chain-link fence. Long rows of colorful Christmas lights hung over the lot, strung from white wooden posts that were wrapped with red ribbon–like peppermint sticks.

There was an aluminum-sided trailer parked near the lot's entrance with various-sized wreaths hanging from pegs on the front of it, all marked with price tags.

Music was playing from a PA system, but it wasn't Christmas music. It was seventies rock. "Take the Long Way Home" by Supertramp. *Who still listens to Supertramp?*

Business seemed light (who shops for a

Christmas tree at three in the afternoon?), and there were only a few cars parked outside the fence.

I walked through the front entrance into the makeshift forest. There were four other customers inside the fenced area, an elderly couple and an older man with what was likely his grandson. A young, skinny man wearing a denim jacket over a hoodie passed by me dragging a tree toward the entrance. He was followed by the elderly couple.

"Can I help you with something?" he asked as he walked by.

"I'm looking for a tree," I said.

"Be right with you."

"I've got it, Shelby," another voice said.

I turned to see an attractive man walking toward me. He looked to be about my age, early thirties, with striking brown eyes beneath thick eyebrows. His hair was dark brown, short but combed back, half-hidden beneath a wool cap. His face was covered with a partial beard, kind of an extended goatee, though along his jawline it was not more than stubble, as if it had either just started to grow or he was trying to look like Hugh Jackman.

I had never seen Clive with facial hair. I'm not even sure he could grow a beard. Once when I'd suggested he attempt to grow one, he said, "No one trusts a politician with a beard." When I countered that Lincoln had had a beard, he replied, "Yeah, and look how that turned out."

Frankly, when it comes to facial hair and politicians, it's the mustache that should be feared. Stalin and Hitler had particularly memorable lip hair.

He smiled as he approached me. "Hi, I'm Andrew. May I help you?"

I felt butterflies. "Hi. I'm . . . I need a tree."

"I suspected that," he said with a half smile. "Not that I'm psychic."

I felt stupid. "I guess most people coming here want a tree."

"Unless they're lost," he said. "What kind of tree are you looking for?"

"Kind?"

"Most people have a favorite. It's usually what they grew up with. Norway spruce, Nordmann fir, blue spruce, Fraser fir, Douglas fir, lodgepole pine . . ."

The names were lost on me. I pointed to the one closest to me. "What kind of tree is that?"

"That's a Fraser fir."

"Is it good?"

"All the trees I sell are good."

"I mean, are some better than others?"

"That depends on what you're looking for. Like, do you want a tree with a nice smell or something that's a little lower-maintenance?"

"Lower-maintenance is good. I don't need

anything dying on me," I added. "Enough has died in my life this year."

He looked at me empathetically and said, "Low maintenance. Then we'll stay away from this one." He stepped away from a nearly perfectly cone-shaped tree.

"But I liked that one," I said.

"You won't after you get it home. That's a Norway spruce. It's a pretty tree, but it has sharp needles, which it loses fairly fast. Unless you like vacuuming every day, but you said you wanted low maintenance."

"Definitely low maintenance," I said.

"How tall a tree were you thinking?"

"Just regular."

His brow fell. "Regular. How high is your ceiling?"

"I don't know. Normal."

He grinned lightly. "Regular and normal. Is your ceiling eight or nine feet?"

"I really don't know."

"What year was your house built?"

"What does that have to do with my tree?"

"Before 1995 most ceilings were eight feet. In the next decade, they changed to nine. Is it a new home?"

"It's an older house. I think it was built in the seventies."

"The golden years. So, you need a six-foot tree. You want to allow room for a star."

"I don't have a star."

"Or whatever. Not everyone puts a star on top of their tree. I've seen spires, cones, snowflakes. I've even seen a Death Star."

"I was just thinking how much I wanted a Death Star on my tree," I said sardonically.

"I might have a Yoda topper. Put me on a tree, you will."

I grimaced. "Was that your Yoda imitation?"

"Sadly," he replied.

"I want a tree that's sturdy," I said. "And cute. Not one of those asymmetrical ones. Something well-rounded."

"Cute, sturdy, six foot, and well-rounded. You're still describing a tree here?"

"Yes." I smiled, a surprising blush creeping down my neck. I pointed at a tree. "How about that one?"

He walked over to it. "This would be a good choice for you. It's a balsam fir. It's a classic tree with a nice scent and it doesn't lose its needles as fast as some of the others. Its only downside is that it's not great for heavy ornaments because its branches aren't real thick."

"I don't have heavy ornaments. How much is it?"

He pulled out a tape measure and measured the tree. "They're nine dollars a foot, so this is fifty-four dollars. I'll make it fifty even."

"Thank you," I said. "I'll take it."

He reached in to the tree's trunk and lifted it. I followed him as he carried my tree to a long worktable surrounded by piles of sawdust.

"I'm going to give it a fresh cut. That will help it live longer."

"I could use a fresh cut," I said beneath my breath. He furtively glanced over at me, then placed the tree up on the table with the tree's trunk hanging over the side. He donned plastic safety glasses, then fired up a chainsaw, its squeal drowning out all other sound. Cutting trees was something my father was always doing. I tried to imagine Clive holding a chainsaw, but I couldn't. His hands were too soft.

Andrew cut off the bottom three inches of the tree, then killed the chainsaw engine and brought the tree over to me. "She's ready to go."

"The tree is three inches shorter now," I observed.

"Yes?"

"That's like two dollars' worth of tree." I was only joking, but he didn't catch it.

"I'll make it forty-five," he said. "Do you need anything to go with it?"

"Like what?"

"Do you have a tree stand?"

"I think so. It's probably in our shed. If I can find it. I'm not sure where my husband—my ex-husband kept it."

He nodded calmly. "Well, you'll need one. If

you want, I can get you one, then you can bring it back when you find yours."

"That works."

"What kind would you like?"

"Just pick one for me."

From the side of the trailer he lifted a large green stand that looked like an impaled plastic pail with aluminum pole legs. "I like these; they're big, but they hold a lot of water, so you can water every few days and not worry about it drying out. Do you need lights?"

"No. We've got a million of them. I mean, I do. Now." I sounded stupid.

"All right." He added up the amount on a tablet. "That will be fifty-five dollars with your discount. With tax, that's fifty-eight forty-three. The stand was ten."

"Thank you, but you don't really have to give me the discount. I was just kidding."

"It's done," he said. I pulled out my wallet and handed him my credit card. He ran it through a card reader, then handed me the iPad. "If you'll autograph that. You can use your finger to sign."

I signed it and handed it back.

"Thank you," he said. "You're parked out front?"

"Just outside your gate."

"If you'll take the tree stand, I'll carry the tree out for you."

I took the stand, which was heavier than I

expected. He grabbed a ball of twine, got my tree, and followed me to my car. As I unlocked my front door, he stopped about ten feet behind me.

"That's your car?"

I was used to people taking jabs at the size of my vehicle. "Yes."

"It's a little . . . little."

"I prefer *fun-sized*. Besides, it gets forty miles to a gallon and I can park it anywhere."

"That's good," he said, "because parking it would be a lot safer than driving it. You could hit a squirrel and total it."

I bit back a smile. "Now you're mocking me."

"Mocking aside, tying the tree to your car isn't going to work real well. And by real well, I mean it's not going to work."

"Well, it's all I've got. Maybe I should have gone with one of those fake trees you can pull apart."

He shook his head. "Fake trees are for underachievers. Do you know anyone with a truck?"

"The FedEx guy."

A smile flitted across his face. "Where do you live?"

"About four miles from here. Over by the Target."

He glanced back at the lot. "We close at eight

tonight. If you don't mind waiting, I can drive it over after we close. If that's not too late."

"How much will that be? To deliver it."

"A cup of coffee."

I liked the price. "Deal." I wrote down my address and handed it to him. "I will see you between eight and eight thirty. After that, I'm indisposed."

The corners of his mouth rose. "Then I'll try to be there before you're indisposed."

I got in my car, glanced at him in the rearview mirror, and pulled out onto the slushy street. I was glad he was coming to my house.

CHAPTER
Twelve

I invited a man over for coffee. His name
is Andrew. He is a pleasant stranger.
—Maggie Walther's Diary

Indisposed? Where did that come from? I'm not
sure why I said that. It's not like I had plans. I
supposed that I was protecting myself, but I
wasn't sure from what.

I stopped at the grocery store on the way home
and bought some coffee, chocolate biscotti, and a
few other necessities I'd put off buying. Actually,
I ended up with a cart full of groceries. I hadn't
really been shopping in a while.

I went home and put everything away, then
straightened up the house in anticipation of his
arrival, even lighting the candle my neighbors
had brought me. It made my front room smell
like wassail.

I dragged an upholstered chair from the corner
of the front room to make space for the tree, then
went out to the garage to see if Clive had left our
tree stand there. I couldn't find it, so I placed the
new stand about where I figured the tree would
go.

I thought about the man at the tree lot. Andrew.

He was beautiful, really. But especially his eyes. There was something mesmerizing about his eyes. They were clear but soulful, maybe even sad—an irony in light of his obvious sense of humor and contagious smile.

I made myself a vegetable omelet for dinner, started a fire in the front room's gas fireplace, then picked up a book and sat down on the couch to read as the grandfather clock in the foyer chimed six.

It was two hours past dark when a red truck with a yellow snowplow stopped in front of my home, backed up, and then pulled into my driveway. I could see Andrew inside. I opened the door and walked outside without my jacket, my arms crossed at my chest to keep myself warm. Andrew looked up at me, shut off his truck, and climbed out.

"You found me," I said, my breath freezing in a cloud in front of me.

"I'm glad you came out. I wasn't sure I had the right place. It's kind of hard finding addresses when the curbs and mailboxes are covered with snow." He walked around to the bed of his truck and dropped the gate. "Should I bring it in through the front door?"

"Yes. Do you need any help?"

"No, I've got it." He lifted the tree from the back of the truck and carried it up the walk to my front porch.

"Come on in," I said, stepping inside. "You can just put it there in the corner. Where I put the tree stand."

He stamped his feet on the mat. "I'm going to get your carpet wet. Should I take off my shoes?"

"You're okay," I said.

He carried the tree in, leaving a light trail of needles in his wake. He lifted the tree onto the stand's metal peg and moved it around until it fell into place. Then he stepped back to inspect it. "Perfect." He turned back to me. "It just needs some decorations."

"I can handle that. Thank you for bringing it. How much do I owe you?"

"I think I quoted you a cup of coffee."

I smiled. "Would you like to come into the kitchen while I make it?"

"Sure."

"This way." He followed me into the kitchen. "You can sit at the table."

He pulled out a chair and sat down. "You have a beautiful home."

"Thank you."

"How long have you lived here?"

"A little over three years. I'm going to miss it."

"You're moving?"

"Eventually. This house is too big for just me." I took the pot and poured two cups. "How do you like your coffee?"

"Cream and sugar."

"I've got half and half," I said.

"Even better."

I carried the cups over to the table. I retrieved a pint carton of half and half from the refrigerator and a tin can with sugar cubes from the cupboard next to it, then brought them over to the table and set them next to the cups. I sat down across from him.

"Thank you," he said.

"You're welcome. How often do you make deliveries?"

"Not often."

"Here's your sugar." I slid the tin can to him.

"Then I'm lucky."

"Yes, you are." He lifted a sugar cube out of the can. "They're pink. And heart-shaped."

"I made them with rosewater. Then dyed them."

"You make your own sugar cubes?"

"Doesn't everybody?"

He laughed. "I don't even know anyone who uses them anymore." He lifted one between his thumb and forefinger. "These are . . . awesome. Definitely Martha Stewart."

"By awesome, do you mean an utter waste of time?"

He grinned. "They're art. No time creating art is wasted. They almost look too nice to use."

"They're not," I said.

He dropped two hearts into his cup.

"So, what do you do when you're not selling

Christmas trees? Or is that a full-time gig?"

He smiled. "No, it's something I'm experimenting with. It's only ninety days out of the year. This is my entrepreneurial side. By profession I'm a financial consultant. Or was. I used to own an investment firm, but I let that go when I moved to Utah."

"Where did you come from?"

"Colorado."

My thoughts bounced immediately to Clive's extraneous Colorado family. I pushed the thought away.

"Why did you come to Utah?" I asked.

"A change of scenery," he said. "I had some bad things happen to my business, followed by a painful divorce."

"I'm sorry," I said. "We've got that in common. At least the divorce part. Where did you move from?"

"Just outside Denver. Thornton."

What are the chances? I thought. It was the same town where Clive's second family lived. I wondered over the vague possibility that he knew the woman. Again I pushed away the thought. "So how is the Christmas tree business?" I asked.

"It's all right. I'm not going to pay off the national debt with my profits, but I'll put a little away. Then onto the next thing."

"And what is that?"

"I'm not sure yet. I'm thinking of starting my firm up again."

"Is that difficult?"

"Yes. But I was pretty good at it. I had it up to thirty million before things went south."

I looked at him in surprise. "Thirty million . . . dollars?"

"If it were pesos, it wouldn't have been as impressive."

I sipped my coffee. "You said some bad things happened to your business."

"Horrible things," he said. "Nothing I'd want to ruin our time together sharing. What do you do?"

"I own a catering business."

"Which explains the fancy sugar cubes. What kind of catering?"

"Weddings, personal, corporate. An occasional movie production. Pretty much the whole gamut."

"You must be busy this time of year."

His words tweaked me a little with guilt, reminding me that Carina was working seventy-hour weeks. My absence was putting a lot of extra pressure on her. "We're swamped. Business is good."

"Good," he said. He finished his coffee.

"Would you like some more?"

"Thank you," he said, "but I'd better let you go; you said you were busy."

Disappointment washed over me. Still, he

hadn't moved from his chair. "No worries. I'm okay on time. Thank you for bringing the tree. I wasn't even going to get one this year. I haven't been in a celebrating mood."

"I understand. I still don't have a tree myself."

"You sell them, but you don't have one?"

"You know how it is—the cobbler's children have no shoes. Besides, it's just me."

"It's just me too," I said.

"So what changed your mind about getting a tree?"

"A friend of mine. She thought it might help me emotionally to decorate for the season. You know, to get in the spirit of Christmas."

"Is it working?"

"Apparently. I'm not balled up in a fetal position somewhere."

He looked at me sympathetically. "Life can be hard. And the holidays seem to amplify whatever pain we're going through."

"They can," I said. I took a drink from my coffee, then suddenly blurted out, "So, you probably heard about my husband. It was all over the news."

He shook his head. "I'm sorry, I don't watch much news."

"Have you heard the name Clive Walther?"

"No. Should I have?"

"That's refreshing. You're probably the only one in Utah who hasn't heard of him."

"Well, I'm new here."

"Then I should probably tell you."

He looked at me for a moment, then asked, "Why?"

It was a good question. Here he'd sat down to enjoy some coffee and pleasant conversation, and now I was going to vomit all over him my tragic marriage.

"Is it something you want to talk about?"

I wasn't sure how to answer. It had practically become part of my introduction. *Hi, I'm Maggie Walther. My husband had another wife and family.*

"No," I said. "Not really."

"We don't need to talk about anything that brings you pain," he said, his eyes kind.

"Thank you."

The moment stretched awkwardly. I couldn't think of anything else to say. Finally, he said, "Well, I probably should go. I still need to count up the day's receipts."

"Of course," I said, silently berating myself over our conversation. "I didn't mean to keep you."

"I'm glad you did. I enjoyed talking. And the coffee."

He stood and we walked together to the front door, stopping on the threshold.

"Thank you for bringing my tree. It looks beautiful."

"A beautiful woman should have a beautiful tree," he said. The compliment was a little corny but still made me feel good. "Good night."

"Night," I said.

It was probably only fifteen degrees out, but I stood in the open doorway watching as he walked out to his truck and started it up. I waved and he waved back. Then he backed out of my driveway and I watched until he turned the corner and his taillights disappeared.

I hoped it wouldn't be the last time I saw him.

CHAPTER
Thirteen

I went back to get Christmas lights. No, actually, that was my excuse for going back to see Andrew. If you can't be honest in your own diary, you should be a novelist and get paid for writing fiction.
—Maggie Walther's Diary

FRIDAY, NOVEMBER 11

Two things were different the next morning. And, after the rut I'd been in, I figured anything different was good. First, the house smelled like pine. It smelled alive again.

Second, I couldn't get Andrew off my mind.

Yesterday had been a good day—the first in a very long string of bad ones. I had had two positive human interactions: first the Stephenses, then Andrew.

I decided to build on my momentum by decorating the tree. The Christmas baubles were in the downstairs storage room with the wrapping paper and Christmas books, but the Christmas lights were all back in the shed.

I looked outside the kitchen window over my

backyard. Icicles hung from the garage and shed roof, some as thick as a cow shank. (I'm not sure why I used that simile. It was something my dad would have said.)

I hadn't braved my backyard since the first storm hit in mid-October. The snow level had only risen since then, piled more than three feet high in some places. From where I was, the shed looked a mile away, sealed by snow drifts halfway up the door. *It would take snow shoes just to get to it,* I thought. *And a pick to chip the ice and snow from the door. Maybe a flamethrower.* At least, that's what I told myself as I got in my car and drove back to the Christmas tree lot.

The truth was thinly veiled in my own mind. I knew why I was going. I wanted to see him again.

As I pulled into the Kroger's parking lot, I looked for his red truck but didn't see it. I parked near the entrance and walked in.

This time I was the only customer in the lot. There were two young men sitting on vinyl folding chairs next to a barrel with a fire inside, the flames occasionally rising above the barrel's rim. Both of them were vaping.

I recognized one of the men from the day before, the guy who had dragged a tree past me. His hair was tied up in a man bun.

When he saw me he pulled his earbuds out,

set his vape down on a box near the chair, and walked up to me. "Hey. May I help you?"

"Is Andrew here?"

"No. The boss doesn't work weekends."

"Oh," I said. "Will he be back on Monday?"

"Sometimes Monday night. It depends when he gets back in town. Tuesday morning for sure. He's on the schedule." He looked me over in a way that made me feel a little uncomfortable. I wasn't old enough to be his mother, but definitely a younger aunt.

"I'm Shel," he said, pushing his hands into his coat pockets. "You were here the other day."

"Yes. Andrew delivered a tree to my house."

"I gotcha," he said. "Is there a problem?"

"No problem."

"I'm in charge when the boss is gone. If you need something, I can help you."

"Thank you. I'm fine," I said. "I just needed to talk with Andrew."

"Cool," he said. "I gotcha. Tuesday morning's your best bet."

"Thanks," I said.

He walked back to his chair near the fire and lifted his vape to his lips. I was surprised at how disappointed I felt as I walked back to my car.

I started driving downtown to the bakery, an old house in the Sugar House area that had been converted to a kitchen and storefront. But, as my building came into sight, I changed my mind.

77

Going in would unleash a multitude of questions and problems I wasn't up to confronting. I turned around and drove home, back to my isolation. At least, this time, I had something to look forward to.

CHAPTER
Fourteen

Did I ask him on a date? I think I did.
> —Maggie Walther's Diary

I got up early Tuesday morning thinking of Andrew, which, frankly, was a whole lot better than thinking of Clive or the drama surrounding him. I wondered if Andrew had even given a second thought to our visit. What if he hadn't? *What if he didn't even remember me?* The thought of that made me feel pathetic, but not enough to keep me from walking into the lot.

I spied Andrew almost immediately. He was standing near the east side of the lot, helping a family with two young children who were so bundled up for winter they looked like Easter eggs.

Andrew noticed me and, to my relief, waved me over.

When I got to him he turned from the family, who were still examining a tree. "Don't tell me your tree died already."

"No, it survived the weekend. But I can't get to my lights. You have Christmas lights, don't you?"

"More than you need," he said. "Let me finish up here and I'll help you."

As he went back to the family, I wandered around the lot looking at the trees, hoping that I wouldn't see one I liked more than the one I had already bought. I was just that way.

Shelby again asked if he could help me. I told him I would wait.

Ten minutes later Andrew found me near the front of the lot. "Thanks again for the coffee the other night."

"Thanks again for bringing my tree," I replied.

"My pleasure," he said. "So, you've decided you need lights after all."

"Mine are buried in my shed. I couldn't get to them."

"Do you know what kind you want?"

"Pretty ones."

He smiled. "I have those. Come with me." I followed him over to the trailer that he used as an office. We stopped in front of an array of lights. "We've got five-millimeter LED lights on green wire, the M-six mini LED lights, the Icicle LED lights, and the C-nine ceramic warm light twinkle bulbs." He stood pleasantly close to me as he pointed out my different options. He smelled like pine and wood shavings.

"Whatever happened to just lights?" I asked.

"We live in a complicated world," he said.

"Which would you buy?"

"Do you know what color you want?"

"Something cheerful."

"Cheerful and pretty." He grabbed a box of lights. "I would recommend our five-millimeter multicolor LED color-morphing lights."

"That sounds exciting," I said.

"Breathtaking," he replied. "More fun than a Christmas tree owner should have. They're constantly changing colors, so with one hundred lights per strand, you never have the same tree twice."

"I'm not sure I could stand that much excitement."

"I'll tell you what. Take them home for a spin. If they're too much of a thrill, bring them back and I'll refund your money, no questions asked."

"Really? No questions?"

"Ne'er a one."

"All right. I'm sold. How many boxes of these miracle lights do I need?"

"The rule of thumb is about a hundred lights for every foot and a half of tree, so yours was six feet, minus the three inches I shorted you, that's about four hundred lights. Four strands."

"How much are they?"

"With the friends and family discount," he said, "just ten dollars a box. They're usually seventeen."

"Thank you," I said, handing him my credit

card. "Does that include installation?" The words tumbled out of my mouth.

"No," he said. "That's extra."

"How much this time?"

He smiled, and my heart jumped. "Dinner."

I smiled back. "Dinner. It's a deal."

"Dinner it is." He ran my card and gave me a slip to sign. "When would you like me to come over?"

If I didn't want to look too eager, I completely blew it. "Is tonight too soon?"

"Tonight's good. My schedule is as open as a politician's mouth."

I don't think he had any idea how relevant his simile was to me. "Mine's pretty open too."

"I've got my other guy back, so I can leave a little early."

"What's a little early?"

"Around seven."

"Seven works. Do you like pasta?"

"I'm a quarter Italian. Pasta is my life force." He put the boxes of lights into a sack and stepped out of the trailer. "I'll carry the lights out to your car. They might fit."

"I don't know why everyone gives me grief about my car."

"Because they can." At the car he said, "Do you want them in the back?"

"The passenger seat is fine." I opened the door. He reached over and set the boxes of lights on the seat, then stepped back. "Great. I'll see you tonight at seven."

"Great," I said back. I hesitated, then said, "Friday night was unexpected. I had a really good time talking to you. It's been a while . . ."

"I was thinking the same thing. I don't have any friends here, really. Just some employees who would rather be playing video games."

I wasn't sure what else to say. "Well, thank you. I'll see you tonight." I climbed inside my car and he shut the door.

"Ciao," he said.

I drove home. It was the happiest I'd felt in months.

CHAPTER
Fifteen

It feels good to be cooking again—
figuratively as well as literally.
—Maggie Walther's Diary

I stopped at the grocery store on the way home and bought everything I needed for dinner, then spent the rest of the afternoon cooking. It felt good to be in the kitchen again. Normalcy. I even made a tiramisu for dessert, one of Marge's recipes. I finished cooking around five. I took a quick nap, then freshened up and set the table.

Andrew arrived about five minutes before seven, carrying a brown paper bag. I opened the door as he walked up. "Come in."

"Thank you."

He stepped inside and pulled the bottle from the sack. "I brought some wine. Antinori Marchese. It's a Chianti."

"Thank you," I said. "I can't wait to try it."

"Whatever you're baking, it smells delicious."

"It's mushroom sausage ragù. And *arancini di riso*."

"*Arancini di riso?*"

"Little oranges. They're deep-fried rice balls full of meat and mozzarella."

"Shall we do the tree first or eat?"

"Definitely eat," I said. "I still need to boil the pasta. I wanted it fresh. In the meantime, I have antipasti."

He followed me back into the kitchen and I offered him a plate of salami, cheeses, and crackers with little pieces of honeycomb. He seemed pleased. "Where did you get this salami?"

"There's a little Italian deli not far from here. Granato's."

"I've driven by that," he said. "I've wanted to stop in but haven't yet. And the honeycomb?"

"The same. The deli owner keeps bees."

"I kept bees once. Like, ten years ago. I thought it might be therapeutic."

"Was it?"

"I learned there's nothing therapeutic about being swarmed by a thousand bees. It's what nightmares are made of."

I laughed. "Why did you think it would be therapeutic?"

"I read an article in the *New Yorker*. Some Madison Avenue executive was extolling the Zen-like experience of beekeeping. I fell for it. One of my employees at the time, Beatrice, had parents who were beekeepers, so she offered to help."

"Her parents kept bees and they named their daughter Beatrice?"

He nodded. "Unfortunately," he said. "I was

out of town when my bees came in, so I asked my brother to pick them up without telling him what they were. He called me from the store, panicked. 'You didn't tell me I was getting bees.' I said, 'I know. I figured you might not do it if I told you.' When he tried to get out of it, I told him to quit being such a baby.'"

"So you shamed your brother into picking up your bees," I said.

"Basically. At least it worked. They came in a little plywood carton about the size of a shoebox. Most of it was screen and you could see the bees in a huge buzzing cluster inside. He was terrified.

"After I got back, Beatrice came over. We dressed up in our bee suits, then she helped me introduce the bees to the hive.

"I was surprised that they were so docile. My ego misread this to believe that I had some special power, like I was a bee whisperer or something. I even got brave enough to take off one of my gloves. Not a single sting. I told Beatrice that I thought the bees knew I meant them no harm and I probably wouldn't even need the suit in the future. She smiled and said, 'You might want to rethink that.'

"I asked her where the queen was, and she pointed to a matchbox-sized box connected to the top of the larger box. The little box was also mostly screen with a cork in one end. I said, 'We let her out last?' She said, 'No; if you let her out now, the bees will kill her. They have to get used to her smell.' Then she pulled out the cork and replaced it with one of those tiny marshmallows. She said, 'By the time she eats her way out, the bees will be used to her smell and accept her as queen.'

"We set the little box inside the hive, covered the hive with a cloth, and left. A week later I came back with my brother. He wanted to watch, but he kept his distance. I had told him how much the bees liked me and that I really didn't need the suit. I lifted the top of the hive and the bees went nuts. They swarmed me. I'm standing there covered with bees and screaming while my brother laughed and recorded it on his phone. He thought it was hilarious. So did the Internet. It went viral. It had like two hundred thousand views."

"Now I have to see that," I said.

"I made him take it down," he said. "I called Beatrice and asked why the change. At first she said, 'They're women, they get moody.' Then she laughed and said, 'When we introduced them to the hive, they didn't have anything to protect. When you went back, they had honeycomb, and babies, and a queen."

"So is that why you quit?" I asked.

"Actually, *they* quit me. One day I went out to the hive and they were gone. All five thousand of them. The queen left and took her friends with her. I took it personally. I mean, I introduced them, bought them a home, fed them, and they left me. I told myself it was them, not me."

I laughed. "Of course it was."

"Then after my wife left me, I figured it really was me."

He makes me happy, I thought. I cooked the pasta for a few more minutes, then fished out a noodle with a fork and tried it. "Al dente," I said. "It's ready." I poured the noodles into a colander, then put them in a bowl and brought them over to the table. After I sat down, Andrew opened the wine and poured our glasses.

"What should we toast?" he asked.

"You brought the wine. You decide."

He thought for a moment, then said, "How about loneliness."

"Loneliness?"

"If it wasn't for loneliness, you probably wouldn't have asked me to stay for coffee."

"Well, if we're taking that route, then we should toast my Fiat as well. Because if I was driving an SUV, there would have been no reason for you to come over."

He smiled. "All right, to your Fiat. May it never encounter anything larger than itself."

"Amen," I said.

We clinked our glasses, then savored the wine. It was delicious, fruity with a hint of chocolate and anise. Perfect for the meal.

We ate a moment in silence. I'm not sure why, but I suddenly felt shy. I hadn't been on a first date in more than a decade. *Was* this a first date?

"You're a good cook," he said, breaking the silence. "Of course you are. You're a professional."

"Thank you."

"Do you like cooking? I mean, it's your business, which means either you're living your passion or you're sick of it by now."

"Yes," I said.

He smiled and nodded.

"Do you cook?" I asked.

"Some. Lately I eat out a lot, so this is especially nice."

"Do you always go by Andrew?" I asked. "Or do your friends call you Andy?"

"Not if they want to remain friends."

I laughed.

"It's helpful, having a name that people want to abbreviate. People used to call my office and try to bypass my secretary by saying they were 'a friend of Andy's.' She'd say, 'If you were really a friend, you'd know he never goes by Andy. Good-bye.'"

"So it was like a secret password."

"Exactly. How about you? Is Maggie your name, or is it an abbreviation of Margaret?"

"Actually, neither," I said. "It's complicated. My real name is Agnetha."

"Agnetha. That sounds Norwegian. Is it a family name?"

"It's Swedish. And no, it's not family. My father was a fan of the Swedish band ABBA. Do you know ABBA?"

He nodded. "Agnetha was the cute blonde."

"My dad had a crush on her, so I got her name. Growing up in Oregon with the name Agnetha didn't work real well, so everyone started calling me Aggie. Then after I moved here, I learned that the Utah State sports teams are called the Aggies. After a year I got tired of being reminded that I shared the name with their blue bull mascot, so I added an *M*. Like I said, it was complicated."

"I've always thought of names as fluid," he said.

"Really?"

"Absolutely. I think everyone should have at least a couple of aliases."

"Do you?"

He looked at me with a peculiar grin. "Absolutely. So what should I call you?"

"Maggie," I said, glad that he asked the question.

"Maggie it is."

We quietly ate for a while, and then I said, "Do you mind my asking what happened to your marriage?"

"My marriage," he said with a sigh. "I guess she

found out that I wasn't as great as she thought."

"She must have had unreasonably high expectations."

"Thank you," he said. "I tried to tell her that. She just wasn't having it."

I laughed. "I'm sorry."

"I should have seen it coming. You should never marry someone who is better-looking than you are. She was a full point and a half ahead of me on the Standard Attraction Scale."

"The Standard Attraction Scale? I didn't know there was such a thing."

"Oh, it's real. It was established by a grant from the Coco Chanel Looks Matter Foundation." I laughed again. He continued. "See, if I were smart, I'd get up and walk out that door right now, because you're at least a point and a quarter above me."

I grinned. "Only a point and a quarter? So you're saying your ex-wife was prettier than I am?"

He grimaced. "Yikes. I walked right into that one. And no, I may have exaggerated her a little."

I smiled at him. "You make me happy."

"At least I'm making someone happy. After she left me, she married a rich guy who looked like a young George Clooney. She was always looking for the BBD."

"What's the BBD?"

"The bigger, better deal."

"Oh." I took a bite of pasta and followed it with a sip of wine. I thought Clive was my BBD. "For the record, I think you're better-looking than George Clooney."

"Now you've lost all credibility. But thank you for trying to flatter me."

"I'm not flattering. I meant it."

"Thank you," he said. "So what was your ex's Standard Attraction Score?"

"Clive, my ex, was handsome in a Ken doll sort of way, if that's what you're into."

"Is that what you're into?" he asked.

"I thought I was."

"And now?"

I grinned, swirling my wine in its glass. "Maybe clean-cut isn't the way to go."

He looked like he was thinking. "So if he's a Ken doll, what does that make me?"

"You're more like a G.I. Joe. The one with the beard."

"Nice," he said. "I had one of those when I was a boy. A G.I. Joe with lifelike hair. And kung fu grip."

"I've always wanted a man with kung fu grip."

Andrew laughed. "Speaking of martial arts, how long were you married?"

"Nine years. But I should have known it was doomed from our honeymoon."

"Why is that?"

"It was a train wreck. Clive wanted to take me

to Taiwan, where he had served a church mission. I personally wanted something more romantic, but he was insistent.

"First, our flight out of San Francisco was canceled, so we ended up sitting in the airport for fourteen hours. Then we got rerouted to Japan, where we got stuck because a typhoon hit. We ended up waiting four days in a hotel in Tokyo, then flew back home because we were out of time and Clive was starting a new job. The fates were against us from the beginning."

"I can beat your honeymoon disaster," he said.

"You can beat a typhoon?"

He nodded. "Oh, yeah. Jamie and I had the worst honeymoon ever. In fact, it's so bad, someone could write a book about it."

"What kind of book?"

"A tragicomedy."

"This sounds interesting. Tell me."

"All right. So, Jamie's dream honeymoon was Bora Bora. You've seen the pictures—perfect Windex-blue water, white sand beaches, thatched huts."

"Which is what I wanted," I interjected.

He smiled. "Right. Well, I went one further and got us a place on a private island. To get there you had to go by boat."

"Sounds dreamy," I said.

"You would think," he replied. "As our boat

approached the island, the first thing we saw was a woman standing on the dock wearing pink cowboy boots."

"Cowboy boots?"

"Pink ones. And nothing else."

"Oh, my."

"She was obviously some kind of model. I mean, she looked photoshopped. Then another nude model walked out. It turned out that I had booked the resort at the exact same time that *Playboy* magazine had planned their 'Girls of Bora Bora' issue. They took over the entire island. Every restaurant, every beach, no dress code. No shirts, no shoes, no problem."

"I'll bet you just hated that."

"Think about it," he said. "We're on our *honeymoon*. Jamie kept telling me she felt like chopped meat. So I'm dealing with massive insecurity and trying to pretend that I see nothing. We ended up spending almost all our time in our room, with Jamie looking at herself in the mirror and accusing me of looking at other women. After that, she didn't talk to me for days."

"You're right," I said. "You have the typhoon beat."

He took a drink of wine, then looked back at me. "May I ask you something about your divorce? You don't have to answer."

"I doubt it's something I haven't been asked before."

"I was just wondering if he filed for divorce or you did."

"I did. But it was because of something he did."

"He cheated?"

"I wish it were that simple. He took it to the next level. Are you sure you've never heard of my husband?"

He shook his head. "Clive Walther? I think I would remember that name."

"He didn't just have another woman, he had a whole other family in Colorado."

His brow furrowed. "Where in Colorado?"

"Thornton."

"My Thornton?" I nodded. He thought for a moment, then said, "Wait. He wasn't a politician—"

"He was a city councilman."

Andrew sighed. "I guess I did hear something about that. I'm so sorry."

"It's just so embarrassing."

"It is for him."

"It is for me too. People think I'm either a loser or stupid."

He looked at me quizzically. "What people?"

"You know." I flourished my hand through the air. "Them."

"You mean, the *public?*"

"Yes."

He set his napkin on the table. "You know public opinion is a vapor, right? Today's hero is tomorrow's loser and vice versa. And those who are shouting the loudest are usually those living the most desperate lives. They're just glad that someone came along who is having a worse week than they are.

"Second, the public has the attention span of a goldfish. I know what happened must seem like the end of the world to you, but that's because you're in the path of the storm. Trust me, they've already moved on to the next drama."

Oddly, it was the most comforting thing anyone had said to me yet. "I hope you're right."

He looked at me seriously. "I know I'm right. I've been there."

"You've been in the middle of a public scandal?"

He hesitated for a moment, then said, "Yes. But it was business-related, not family. I'm sorry that you had to share your heartbreak in the media. I think they forget that there are real people involved."

"Forget, or don't care?" I said.

"Maybe both," he said. "I'm sorry."

"This will pass," I said. "At least, that's what I keep telling myself."

Andrew frowned. "I'm sorry I brought it up. I'd like you to think of me as someone who makes you happy."

"You do make me happy."

"Good. No more talk of drama."

"I can do that," I replied.

We went back to eating. When he finished his pasta, he asked for more, which made me glad. As he was finishing I said, "I made tiramisu for dessert."

"I love tiramisu," he said.

"Good, because I made a whole pan, and I'm sending the leftovers home with you."

I got up and took our plates to the counter, cut us two rectangles of tiramisu, and brought them over to the table. He took a bite and said, "Perfect."

"Do you know what *tiramisu* means?"

"No idea."

"In Italian, *tira* means to lift or pick up, *mi* means me, and *su* means up. So it literally is a pick-me-up."

"Because of all the espresso in it."

"Exactly," I said. "The magic of caffeine."

"Now that I have all this caffeine in me," he said, "should we do the dishes?"

"I can handle them," I said.

"I know you can handle them, but should we do the dishes?"

"You're sure you have time?"

"I've got nothing but time."

"All right," I said, "you can help. You wash, I'll dry and put them away."

Andrew began clearing the table while I filled the sink with hot water. As I handed him a dish, he looked at my left hand. "Why are you still wearing your wedding ring?"

I shrugged. "I just never took it off." I glanced down at my ring, a simple white-gold band with a half-carat marquise diamond. "Maybe it's the same reason people wear cloves of garlic around their necks."

"Who wears cloves of garlic around their necks?"

"People who are afraid of vampires."

"Are you comparing men to vampires?"

"Some are," I said. "I've even met a few female vampires."

"I bet you have."

"The way I see it, everyone has good and bad in them. Some just have more of one than the other." I looked at him. "Unless they're bloodsucking vampires."

He nodded. "Unless they're bloodsucking vampires."

We both laughed. Then I looked into his eyes. "Are you a vampire?"

He met my gaze. "A real vampire would never answer that question in the affirmative. What do you think?"

I shook my head. "I think . . . you're sweet."

To my surprise, his mouth twisted in disappointment. "Sweet. Like a girlfriend is sweet?"

"There's nothing girlfriend about you," I said. As I looked at him I suddenly wanted him to kiss me. I hoped he was thinking the same. He smiled at me, handed me a plate, and said, "Last one. How about I finish drying and you put things away?"

I breathed out slowly. "It's a plan."

We finished up in the kitchen and went out to decorate the Christmas tree.

I said, "We put the lights on first?"

"Yes, but first we make sure the lights work."

"Good idea. The guy who sold them to me was kind of sketchy."

He grinned. "Yeah. I've never trusted drifters who work at Christmas tree lots."

He laid out the boxes, opened them, then carefully laid out the strands in neat rows. "Do you have an extension cord?"

"Yes. I'll get it."

"Maybe we should have some Christmas music. Set the mood."

"I can get that too." I walked down the hall to the closet and grabbed the extension cord. Then I found some instrumental Christmas music on my iPod and plugged it into my stereo in the kitchen. The comforting sound of music filled the house. I went back into the front room. The strands were all connected and laid out in order. I handed him the cord.

"Thank you." He plugged in the lights, and they flashed on. I had forgotten that they changed colors. "They work."

99

"They're pretty."

"That's what you asked for." He starting disconnecting the lights from each other.

"Why are you doing that?"

"Because they're easier to install if you break the tree up into quadrants."

"Do you start from the top or the bottom?"

"Always the top. Because if you get to the top and you have an extra yard of lights, what do you do?"

"You just wrap them around again."

He shook his head. "You are such a novice."

After we had wrapped the lights around the tree, he walked to the center of the room and looked at the tree, squinting.

"What are you doing?" I asked.

"I'm looking for dark holes."

"Why are you squinting?"

"That's the best way to find dark holes."

"You are hard-core," I said.

"No, I'm a professional."

It was after midnight when we finished decorating the tree. Then we sat down on the couch to admire our creation.

"There's something peaceful about a Christmas tree," I said. "When I was little, I would just lay there and look at the tree until I fell asleep in front of it."

He nodded slowly. "What was your childhood like?"

I groaned a little.

"It was bad?"

"Yeah. My father was interesting."

"Interesting unique, or interesting a living hell?"

"The latter, mostly. But he was definitely unique."

"Were you raised in Utah?"

"No. I'm from southern Oregon. A town called Ashland. You probably haven't heard of it."

"I've been there," he said.

"You've been to Ashland?"

"About six years ago I went with my brother to the Shakespeare Festival."

"Ashland's famous for that."

"What did your father do?"

"Pretty much everything. He was a jack-of-all-trades. He came to Oregon when he was nineteen to work in a lumber yard. He ended up owning a lot of land. More than six hundred acres. That was back when it was cheap and before the Californians started moving in," I said, imitating his drawl.

"Is your father still alive?"

"Yes."

"Do you see much of him?"

"I haven't seen him since my wedding. I was surprised that he even came to that."

"What about your mother?"

"She was wonderful. At least what I remember of her. She died when I was fourteen."

"I'm sorry," he said. "Did your father ever remarry?"

"About six years ago. He married a woman a few years younger than me. He made it a point to tell me that he redid his will so everything goes to her when he dies. He owns several millions of dollars' worth of land."

"So he's wealthy?"

"You wouldn't know it. He still lives in the log cabin he built forty years ago."

"He lives in a log cabin?"

"Well, it's not, like, Abraham Lincoln's place. It has plumbing, a Jacuzzi tub and sauna. It's almost three thousand square feet."

"Will he ever sell his land?"

"Not while he's living. It's his refuge. He's a . . . what's the word? Prepper? He has his own well, a shed full of dynamite, and an arsenal. He even makes his own shotgun shells." I groaned again. "He hates the world. And he hates that they're encroaching on him. Especially the environmentalists.

"Once he was clearing some trees on his property and his environmentalist neighbors called the police on him. As soon as the officer left, my father grabbed me and stomped over to their house. My dad's a big man, about six-foot-three, with an even bigger temper.

"In the old days he would have just called out the man—or dragged him out of his house—and beaten him up. But times have changed, and my father's smart enough to know it. He knew his neighbors would sue him, so he used a different strategy.

"He pounded so hard on the door that it shook. When the people came, they only opened the door enough to peer out. I remember how terrified they looked. They asked my dad what he wanted. He calmly said to them, 'You know, you live downwind of me. That eastern ocean wind flows down the mountain slopes like a rushing river.'

"The man said, 'How poetic. What's your point?'

"My father said, 'The next time you meddle in my affairs, I'm going to build a pig farm on the border of our property. Just right there, not twenty yards from your house. You snowflakes ever been to a pig farm?' The woman started making some clueless comment about being vegan and the horrors of the pig-slaughtering industry, and my father said, 'The smell carries for more than a mile, two on a windy day. In the summer it's so dank, you can taste the stink. Just twenty yards away, you're going to think you're living in a pigsty. Your food will taste like pig dung. That's not to mention the flies. The infestation will be biblical. Then I'll slaughter the pigs myself and leave them hanging on meat hooks by your fence. You won't be able to live here and you won't be able to sell your house. Hell, you won't be able to give it away.'

"The man said, 'You can't do that.' My father replied, 'Check the zoning, sweetie.' Then his wife said, 'You wouldn't dare.' My father laughed and said, 'Just try me, you liberal morons. Just try me.' Not surprisingly, they never called the police on him again."

"He sounds like an interesting man," Andrew said. "I'd like to meet him."

"No you wouldn't."

"But he was pretty shrewd."

"He could take care of himself. That's what he was best at." I frowned. "Sometimes I'm glad my mother died young so she didn't have to spend her life with him."

"How old were you when you left home?"

"Eighteen. I was waitressing and a driver told me about Utah. It sounded nice, so I moved here."

"Are you an only child?"

"No. I have a little brother. He's in Alaska working on an offshore oil rig."

"Do you see much of him?"

"No. Maybe every few years. He left five years after my mom died. I don't blame him. My father had registered him for the army so he could steal his girlfriend."

"Your father stole his own son's girlfriend?"

"He tried. That's how he was. After my mother

died, he started dating girls from my high school. I'd be walking home from cheerleading and I'd see him drive by in his Porsche with one of my classmates. If it wasn't such a small town, he probably would have been in jail."

Andrew shook his head. "That's horrific."

"So that's how I ended up in Utah. I came here to go to school, met the owner of a catering business, and ended up owning it."

"You've done well."

"The business does well. Not that I'm much help these days."

"So who runs it?"

"One of my employees. Actually, she's more of a friend than an employee. Her name's Carina. She's worked for me for over five years. When everything came down with Clive, I melted down, and she stepped in and took over. She's overwhelmed, but she doesn't complain." I suddenly yawned. "Sorry."

"It's late," he said.

"I'm okay," I said quickly. "You're the one with a job." I looked into his eyes. "Are you tired?"

"A little. But I don't want to go just yet."

This made me smile. I continued the conversation. "Are your parents still alive?"

"No. My parents died in a car accident when I was young. So my brother and I were raised by my aunt and uncle. They couldn't have children, so they adopted us."

"Are you close to your brother?"

"Very. Not physically, though. He's still in Colorado."

"How often do you see him?"

"Every chance I get."

I yawned again. Then Andrew yawned. We both laughed.

"I'll go," he said.

"All right."

He stood first, then reached down and helped me up from the couch. We walked to the door. "Thank you for dinner. And the conversation. It was delicious."

"Thank you for coming," I said.

He hesitated a moment, then said, "Can I be a little vulnerable with you?"

"Yes."

"After my divorce I told myself that I wouldn't get involved with anyone. But being with you has been nice." He looked vulnerable. Vulnerable and beautiful.

"I know what you mean. I thought it would be a cold day in hell before I spent time with a man."

He grinned. "It's been pretty cold."

"And I've been living in hell," I said. "So I guess it was time." We both smiled. "I guess I didn't realize how lonely I was." I looked into his eyes. "I needed someone kind in my life these days. This is unexpected and welcome."

"If it's okay with you, I'd like to see more of you."

"It's okay with me."

He touched my hair, gently brushing it back from my face. "Can I see you tomorrow?"

"I'd like that."

"What time?"

"Any time. All day if you like."

His smile broadened. "I'd love to, but I'm short on workers tomorrow. What if I came around five and took you to dinner?"

"That sounds nice."

"Do you like sushi?"

"Yes."

"I found a little place up on the Bench. Kobe." He just stood there. Then he leaned forward and lightly kissed me on the lips. I closed my eyes and drank it in. He straightened up. "Good night."

I touched his cheek longingly, then leaned forward and kissed him back. "Good night, Andrew."

He smiled, then turned and walked out the door. I watched him get into his truck, waved, then went inside. It was past two. In spite of the hour, it was the most awake I'd felt in months.

CHAPTER
Sixteen

I saw Clive today. He asked something
big of me. (Bigamy. Yeah, I see it. Not
funny.) I told him no, but I felt so sorry
for him that I could see myself caving.
Sometimes I don't know if I'm an angel
or a doormat.

—Maggie Walther's Diary

I woke the next morning in a pleasant haze.
Happiness. I hardly recognized it. It had been too
long since I'd felt that way. My blissful state was
interrupted by the phone.

"Did I wake you?" Carina asked.

"No, I was up. How was the party last night?"
I'm sure the question surprised her. It was the
first time I'd asked about work in weeks.

"It was crazy. They had double the number of
guests than had RSVPed."

"They should know that no one in Utah RSVPs.
What did you do?"

"Fortunately, we had three sheets of lemon bars
and two sheets of éclairs for tonight's event. So
we used them. The girls are at the house baking
right now."

"I'm sorry I've just dropped this on you."

"Baptism by fire," she said. "It reminds me of how my dad taught me to swim by throwing me into the deep end of the pool."

"Sorry," I said again. "That wasn't my intent."

"I know," she said. She changed the subject. "I came by last night."

"Why didn't you come in?"

"Because there was a truck in the driveway."

"What time did you come by?"

"Around one thirty."

"Why were you driving by my house at one thirty?"

"Because I'm worried about you. I hate that you're all alone. But then I guess you're not."

"I had someone over."

"Who?"

"A guy I just met a few days ago."

"Does he have a name?"

"Andrew."

"You met him after we had coffee?"

"Yes."

"Where did you meet him?"

"Why do I feel like you're interrogating me?"

"Because I am."

"Fair enough. I met him while I was buying a Christmas tree—which, by the way, was your idea."

"Don't blame me . . ."

"I'm not blaming you, I'm giving you credit."

"When I said to change your environment, I meant get a tree, not the guy selling it."

"I thought you'd be happy I wasn't alone. Isn't that what you just said? You hated that I was alone?"

"I do," she said. "It's just that you've only been divorced a few months. You're vulnerable. Just three days ago you were swearing off men, and just like that you have a love interest?"

"I didn't say he was a love interest."

"He was at your house at one thirty."

"Actually, he was there until two," I said.

"Exactly. You're vulnerable. I don't want to see you taken advantage of. How well do you know this guy?"

"I know that he's kind. He's funny, in a subtle way, and he's a great conversationalist."

"How long has he been unemployed?"

"He's *not* unemployed."

"For the *moment*. He works at a Christmas tree lot. Seasonal work. How long was he unemployed before that?"

"He *owns* the Christmas tree lot," I said. "He's an entrepreneur."

"That's a French word for *slacker*."

"I'm an entrepreneur," I said. "He's not a slacker."

"Then why is he single?"

"I'm single, you're single; why would you ask that?"

"Because you and I are nuptial victims."

"So is he. He's divorced."

"How long?"

"I don't know. A few years."

"Where is he from?"

"Colorado. He's been in Utah just a few months. He used to be a financial adviser in Denver. And he's gorgeous."

"Gorgeous?"

"Like, beautiful."

"Now we get to the core of the problem," she said. "Blinded by the hunk."

"I'm done with this conversation," I said.

"Just remember, honey. The nicer the package, the cheaper the gift."

"I am definitely done with this conversation."

"Love you, sweetie."

"Love you too. Have a good day."

In spite of my conversation with Carina, I felt happy all day in anticipation of seeing Andrew again. I didn't disagree with Carina that things were moving fast, warp speed, but after wandering through a desert, when you find water, you don't sip it.

I put on my favorite outfit, something I hadn't worn since before D-Day (Divorce Day). I also spent extra time on my makeup, even plucking my eyebrows, which shows I was motivated.

The clock moved slowly. At a quarter to five my doorbell rang, and my heart jumped a little. I was glad he was early. I quickly opened the door. Clive stood in the doorway.

"Sorry, I left my house key at the police station," he said. "You would think they'd make it a point to return your property."

"Otherwise you would have just walked in?" I asked. Clive didn't respond. "What are you doing here?"

"I need to talk with you."

"About what?"

"It's important."

"*Important?* Like our marriage wasn't?"

"Maggie, don't do this."

I shook my head as I stepped back from the door. "You have ten minutes. I need to be someplace."

"Where?"

"That's not any of your business. And the clock is ticking."

"I don't believe you're timing me." He walked past me to the kitchen. I followed him in as he opened the refrigerator. "Do you have anything to eat?"

"You have nine minutes. What do you want, Clive?"

He grabbed a pear out of the refrigerator, then sat down at the table, gesturing to a seat next to him. I leaned against the counter. "What is it, Clive?"

"I have a court date." He took a bite of the pear. "December fourteenth."

"Congratulations," I said sardonically. "And this has what to do with me?"

"I want you there. By my side."

"You want me to come to court with you?"

He took another bite. "Yes. To show support."

"Why would I do that?"

"To show the jury that I'm not such a bad guy."

"But you are."

"Am I? Wasn't I good to you? Weren't we happy?"

"I thought we were."

"If you think you're happy, you are." He looked at me. "Come on, Maggie. Just this one thing. It's important."

"Why don't you get your other wife to do it? I'm sure she'd be happy to take my place."

"For the record, Jennifer didn't know about you either," he said. "Look, I know I made a mistake."

"A mistake? Taking the wrong exit is a mistake. Taking a second wife is a bit more deliberate."

"Yes, I'm a broken man. I'm a sinner. Is that what you want to hear?"

"I want to hear you leaving my house."

He shook his head. "You mean, the house I bought?"

"The house *we* bought," I said.

He just looked at me. "You know, you used to be nice. You've changed."

"I wonder why."

He was quiet a moment, then said, "Maggie, I really need your help. I could end up in prison. Do this, and I'll make it up to you somehow."

"How?"

"I don't know. What do you want?"

"I want you to leave me out of this."

He sighed. "Mag, how does my going to jail serve the greater good? I know you're angry, but you still have a good heart. You don't want to be responsible for me going to jail."

"Now I'm responsible?" I groaned. "This is just like you, Clive. You're a master at turning things around. That's why you were such a good lawyer."

"Is that a compliment?"

I shook my head. Just then the doorbell rang.

"Expecting someone?" he asked.

"I have a date."

"A date?" He stood, taking his pear. "That didn't take long."

"You need to go."

He just looked at me, then said, "Think about it."

"I don't need to."

"Since when did you become so heartless?"

"If I were heartless, Clive, my heart wouldn't hurt so much."

"I never meant to hurt you."

"Well, you sure didn't mean *not* to."

He threw his hands up in mock surrender.

114

"You're right. You're absolutely right. I never deserved you." He walked to the door, then turned back. "Just because I loved someone else doesn't mean that I ever stopped loving you. I didn't. I still love you. I never wanted the divorce. You know that."

"You had to divorce one of us."

"I don't know why I needed something more. It's something broken in me. I'm getting therapy."

There was a knock on the door.

"You need to leave, Clive."

He breathed out deeply. "Okay. I'll go."

I opened the door. Andrew stood in the doorway. The two men looked at each other.

"Be good to her," Clive said.

"I intend to," Andrew replied.

Clive turned back to me. "Think about it, Mag." He furtively glanced at Andrew, then walked past him to his car. He was driving a new Audi with the paper dealer plates still in the window.

I turned to Andrew. "I'm sorry. Come in."

Andrew stepped inside. "Clive?"

"In the flesh."

Andrew shut the door behind himself. "Are you okay?"

I wasn't sure how to answer. It had been such a shock seeing him. "I'm fine."

He just looked at me. "Are you sure?"

I began to tear up. I quickly brushed a tear from

my cheek. "I don't know if I'm okay." The tears began to fall.

Andrew took my hand. "Come here." He led me over to the couch. We sat down next to each other, our knees touching. He looked into my face. "What did he want?"

"He . . ." I couldn't speak. I just started crying harder. Andrew put his arm around me and pulled me into him. I laid my face on his shoulder and sobbed. For nearly five minutes he just held me, gently running his hand over my back, saying softly, "You're going to be okay."

When I had gained some composure, I looked up into his face. "He wants me to be with him at his trial."

"Why would he ask that?"

"He thinks it will help with the jury."

"I'm sure it will. But why would he think he could ask that of you?"

"Because he knows I will. I always give in to him."

"You don't need to." He looked into my face. "Do you still love him?"

I swallowed. "I don't know. We were married nine years. Is it wrong if part of me still does?"

Andrew slowly shook his head. "There's nothing wrong with that. You're loyal, even if he wasn't. Just don't let him use that against you."

Why is he so kind to me? "Thank you."

He said tenderly, "I worry about you."

"I'm glad you worry about me."

He touched my face softly, stroking my cheek with the back of his hand. "You'll get through this. I promise. I'll help you."

I looked deeply into his eyes. "Will you?"

He nodded. "Yes." His face moved closer to mine, his eyes both wild and soft. I moved forward to meet him, our lips pressing together.

It was bliss, his soft lips and hard, whiskered face against my face. His love felt so sweet. I just wanted to bury all my pain in him. I wanted to escape in him. For the next several hours, I did just that. I couldn't believe what I'd done. I'd fallen in love.

CHAPTER
Seventeen

Andrew invited me on a trip to Mexico.
It's just a trip. Right? It's just a trip. Right.
— Maggie Walther's Diary

I slept in the next morning. I woke hungry for a change. Andrew and I had never gone out to dinner. Instead we had talked until early in the morning. Actually, we had talked and kissed.

My phone vibrated with a text. I rolled over and grabbed it, hoping it was from him. It was. I had also missed a phone call from Carina twenty minutes earlier.

ANDREW
Good morning, beautiful.

I texted back.

MAGGIE
Good morning, handsome. Just woke.
Someone kept me up late.

ANDREW
Who kept you up? Lol.

I thought you might sleep in. I have coffee/ muffin for you. Should I bring them?

MAGGIE
Bring you, please.

ANDREW
On my way.

I lay back in bed. My heart was so full of joy. How long had it been since I'd felt such elation? Ten minutes later my phone vibrated.

ANDREW
I'm at the door.

I pulled on a robe, walked out to the foyer, and opened the door. Andrew was holding a cardboard coffee carrier and a white bakery sack.

"Good morning, beautiful," he said. "May I come in?"

"Anytime," I said.

He stamped off his feet and stepped inside. We kissed, then he said, "Kitchen?"

"Yes, please."

I followed him. He set my coffee on the table along with the paper sack. "I brought muffins. I hope you like muffins."

"How did you know I was hungry?"

"We never went out to eat last night. I kind of felt bad about that."

"Did you hear me complaining?"

He smiled. "Honestly, I didn't feel too bad." He grabbed the sack. "I wasn't sure what kind of muffins you like, so I got almost every kind they had. Banana nut, oatmeal walnut, blueberry, and cinnamon apple. You don't have to eat them all."

"I'll restrain myself. I'll have the apple."

"It's yours," he said, handing me a muffin. "I'll have the blueberry."

We both sat down at the table. "What a nice surprise," I said. "It's almost breakfast in bed."

"That could be arranged," he said.

"So I was thinking, I could make dinner for us tonight. There's this Japanese roast chicken recipe I found. Does that sound good?"

His expression fell. "I can't tonight. I have to leave town."

My heart fell. "Oh. For long?"

"No, just the weekend. I've got to drive to Denver."

"Would you like some company? I don't have any plans."

"Not this time," he said. He must have read the disappointment on my face, because he added, "Maybe next time."

My offer had clearly surprised him. "Is there a next time?"

"I go every week. I have family there that I'm

taking care of." He hesitated. "I'm really sorry. It's been this way since I came to Utah. It should only be a few more weeks."

"It's okay. You don't owe me anything."

"It's not about owing. I want to be with you." He just sat there looking at me. Reading me. "You still look upset."

"I'm sorry. I was just really looking forward to being with you. Last night was so . . ." I didn't finish.

"Amazing," he said. "I'm so sorry. But it's just a day. I'll be back by Saturday night. Then I'll be around for the week."

I think I probably still seemed upset, because he looked at me for a moment, then stood. "Come here."

"Where?"

He put out his hand. "Back to the couch."

"You sound like a psychiatrist."

"Exactly."

I stood and took his hand and we walked back out to the living room. We sat down next to each other on the couch. I draped my arms around him and we kissed. After we parted he said, "Where were we?"

"I was saying that I was looking forward to being with you. I couldn't tell you the last time I was that happy."

"And now I'm depriving you of it."

"Basically," I said, kissing him. We kissed for a

couple of minutes, then I said, "You really want to go? And leave me?"

"No, I don't want to leave you. But I have to." He looked into my eyes. "Don't be blue."

"I'm always blue this time of the year. Why is that?" I said.

"I have no idea."

"You're not much of a psychiatrist."

"No. I'd be horrible at it. Why do you think you're blue this time of year?"

"I think I have that seasonal affect thing."

"SAD," he said. "Seasonal affective disease."

I laughed. "It's *disorder,* not *disease.*"

"You're the one who called it a 'thing.'" He was quiet a moment, then said, "I have a solution, if you're interested."

"You have a solution for my SAD?"

"I do. It's called Los Cabos."

"Cabos? As in Mexico?"

He nodded. "A friend of mine has a condo there. There's no shortage of sun. We should go."

I leaned back to look at him. "Are you serious?"

"Yes. Have you ever been to Cabo San Lucas?"

"No. But I've seen pictures."

"This is the ideal time of the year to go. The weather is perfect and the condo has a perfect view of the ocean."

"You really are serious."

"I am. Is there a problem with that?"

"I barely know you."

"That's true for both of us. Which is why we'll have separate rooms."

"What about your Christmas tree lot?"

"It's November. Sheldon can run it."

"I thought his name was Shelby."

"Whatever," he said.

I laughed. "I can't believe you're serious." My mind reeled at the proposition. "I don't know."

"You said you could use some sun. And I'm betting you could use time out of Utah."

"Both true."

"So why not just say yes?"

"It's just so . . ."

"Spontaneous?"

"Yes. Pisces are not very spontaneous."

"But Pisces are fish and Cabo is on the sea, so it's kind of a natural."

"When would we go?"

"Let me check the flights." He looked at his phone. After some scrolling he said, "There's a direct flight from Salt Lake to Los Cabos Sunday morning."

"You mean Sunday, as in three days from now?"

He nodded. "I'll be back Saturday night. We could stay until Friday morning; that would give us six days."

I thought for a moment. "Wait—it's Thanksgiving that week."

His brow furrowed. "You have plans?"

"Just with Carina. And her parents."

He looked disappointed. "It was a nice thought."

"I could cancel," I said.

"I don't want to get you in trouble with your friend." He smiled. "Or, actually, I do."

"She'll understand. I already felt like a charity case. What about you? Don't you have plans?"

"No, it's just me. I usually spend Thanksgiving in Cabo. Spending Thanksgiving with you would be even better."

I wanted to go more than I could say. "It would be wonderful."

"So?"

"Let's do it," I blurted out.

He glanced down at his phone, then at me. "I'm going to book it. Are you sure?"

I took a deep breath. "Yes."

"And you have a passport?"

"Yes."

He smiled. "Good." He typed into his smartphone and looked up at me. "Done. We're going to Cabo."

"I can't believe I'm doing this. What do I bring? Besides my passport?"

"Just your clothes. Nothing you would wear in Utah right now. Swimsuit, nightwear, sunglasses. The condo has everything we need."

"And you're sure the condo's available?"

He smiled. "Positive."

CHAPTER
Eighteen

Carina's not happy about my impending trip. You would think that I had booked a seat on the *Titanic*.

—Maggie Walther's Diary

"What are you doing, girl?" I said to myself as Andrew drove away. I pulled up the weather app on my phone and typed in Los Cabos. It was sunny with a high of ninety-six degrees. *I know exactly what I'm doing. I'm going to Cabo San Lucas with a complete stranger I've fallen in love with.* A smile crossed my face. I was going to Cabo with a gorgeous stranger. It was the first time that I had something to look forward to in a long, long time.

I couldn't wait to tell someone, which, of course, meant Carina. I sat on the bed and called her. "Hi, doll."

She hesitated. "Maggie?"

"Yes?"

"Wow, I wasn't sure it was you. I haven't heard you this cheery since you found out that dark chocolate is good for you."

"Andrew just invited me to Cabo."

"The Christmas tree salesman?"

"The Christmas tree salesman," I said. "His friend has a condo on the beach and he said we can use it. I checked the weather. It's like ninety-five degrees there today."

"You think that's a good idea?"

"I'll wear sunscreen."

"I meant going to Cabo with a stranger."

"He's not a stranger."

"Uh, he is, Maggie. You've known him like, a week?"

"Eight days," I said. "I'd known you for less than twenty minutes when I hired you. I'm not worried."

"Which is why I am."

"He's a gentleman, Carina. He assured me we'll be staying in separate rooms."

"What do you expect him to say? How do you know he's not dangerous? Mysterious past, just moved to town. A drifter working in a Christmas tree lot—"

"I'm going to pretend that you didn't just say that. He's not a drifter, Carina. He owns the Christmas tree lot. He's contracted with the store."

"Yeah, well, for all you know, he could be a serial killer."

"Now you're being crazy. Besides, he's too sweet."

"Serial killers are always sweet. It's how they lure their victims in."

"Now you're scaring me. Why can't you be happy for me? Last week you were complaining that I was isolating. Now I've found someone and you're unhappy about that."

"That's because it was just last week, Maggie. You don't really know this guy. It's too soon. I just don't want to see your heart getting broken again. You're so vulnerable right now. You're just way too trusting."

"I've never been too trusting."

"Your husband had another family."

I didn't answer. It stung.

"I'm sorry. I shouldn't have said that. I just mean, why don't you spend a little more time getting to know the guy before you run off to another country?"

"Because I like him. Besides, we've already bought the plane tickets."

"Whoa," she said. "You're really doing this. When are you going?"

"Sunday."

"Sunday? When are you coming back?"

I felt a little embarrassed. "We're coming back Friday."

"You're blowing me off for Thanksgiving?"

"I'm sorry. I felt like an imposition."

"Which you're not." She sighed. "All right. I guess I can forgive you. Just don't let him hold your passport. And I want to know the address of this condo."

"I'm telling myself that your paranoia is misguided love."

"It is love. And I want info in case you don't come back."

"If I don't come back," I said, "don't come looking for me."

CHAPTER
Nineteen

Today the Stephenses returned from burying their son. How brightly some people shine in the darkness of adversity.

—Maggie Walther's Diary

Saturday it was snowing again. Andrew called to make sure that I was okay, but, I think mostly to make sure that I hadn't backed out of our trip.

"Nope, you're stuck with me," I said. "Are you in Denver?"

"Yes. Just clearing out of my hotel."

"You don't stay with your family?"

He hesitated. "No, that wouldn't quite work."

"How long does it take to drive to Denver?"

"Driving the legal limit or my limit?"

"Your limit. If you have one."

"A little over seven hours."

"What time will you be home tonight?"

"That depends on the roads. Apparently there's a whiteout right now in Rock Springs. But the roads should be clear by the time I get there."

"It's snowing here too," I said. "You didn't stay very long."

"No. I've only got a small window to visit."

"What do you mean?" I asked.

"It's complicated," he said.

It snowed all day Saturday, which made me even more excited to go to Cabo. It also made me worry about Andrew's drive. I checked the weather in Rock Springs. It looked bad. I was hoping he would make it home in time to come over, but now I was worried he might not make it back at all. At best, he would make it home at two or three in the morning.

The day dragged on. One good thing: I went downstairs and ran on my treadmill. Outside of shoveling snow, I hadn't exercised for weeks. It felt good, though I was amazed at how quickly I was tired.

Around two, my neighbors, the Stephenses, came home. I saw them get out of their car and hold each other as they walked into their house. My heart hurt for them. I put down my book and went to the kitchen and baked them some more cookies. This time I made gingerbread cookies. They were still warm when I walked them over.

Mrs. Stephens answered the door. She recognized me. "How are you, dear?" she asked.

"I'm well," I said. "Thank you. I brought you some cookies."

She glanced at the plate I held. "But you already brought us some. They were a welcome treat to come home to."

"I wanted you to have fresh ones," I said. The truth was, I was afraid that her sister had already eaten them all. "Your sister told me about your son. I'm very sorry."

She looked at me with gray, mournful eyes. "Thank you. He was our only son. A parent shouldn't have to outlive their child."

"I'm very sorry."

"We're grateful that we have the grandchildren. They're going to be moving in with us."

"It's good they have you," I said.

"It's good we have them," she replied. "Our son lives through them." We were both quiet a moment, then she asked, "And how are you doing?"

"I'm doing better. Your coming to help me made a big difference. I was having trouble getting out of the house."

"Well, with all this snow, it's hard for everyone to get out. We've had a lot of snow this year," she said. "I heard on the news it's one of the snowiest winters of the decade."

"I didn't mean the snow," I said. "I just didn't want to go out."

She looked at me thoughtfully, then said, "We were glad to help. If you ever need anything, just call."

"Thank you for being a good neighbor," I said. "Even when I haven't been one."

"You've been busy," she said kindly. "You're at a busy time of life."

"I suppose so."

"Have a nice Thanksgiving," she said. "And thank you again for the cookies. They look exquisite. Bryan will be delighted."

"My pleasure," I said.

I walked back home thinking I would like to be more like her.

I called Andrew around midnight to see if he'd made it back to Salt Lake. Far from it. He told me that the roads had been worse than anticipated and he had just passed Rock Springs, so he wouldn't be home until well past three. He said he'd still be at my house by ten. I told him to be careful.

I woke the next morning feeling anxious. Was it too soon? They say if you really want to get to know someone, you should travel with them. What if Carina was right and he was nothing like I thought he was? What if we didn't get along? I'd be stuck there with him and my flattened heart.

I pushed my worries from my mind. *It's just a trip,* I told myself. And, worst case, at least I'd be out of Utah and the cold. I should have left town long before then.

Anxious or not, I was happy to be leaving town.

CHAPTER
Twenty

They say that if you want to get to know someone, travel with them. Do I really want to know him that well?

—Maggie Walther's Diary

Andrew pulled up to the house a few minutes before ten o'clock. I was sitting in the front room waiting for him. He got out of his truck wearing only a light denim jacket. I put on my ski parka, turned off the lights, and opened the door as he walked up to my porch.

"You're not going to need that coat in Cabo," he said. We kissed.

"I better not," I replied. "It's supposed to be in the nineties."

"I'm ready for it," he said. He opened his jacket. He had on a colorful Hawaiian shirt.

I locked my door. "I'll be ditching the coat the second we're on the plane."

Andrew grabbed my bag and we walked down to his truck. He opened the door for me, put our suitcases in the back seat, and walked around and got in.

Even with slushy roads, the drive to the airport

took only a half hour. We parked in the long-term parking lot and Andrew carried both of our bags to the nearest shuttle stop.

There was one other person at the station—a man standing on the west side of the structure talking on his cell phone. He wore a herringbone peacoat, a long wool scarf wrapped around his neck, and one of those faux fur hats with flaps that fall down over the ears and ties under the chin. His nose was nearly as red as his scarf, and between talking he kept sneezing into a ratty tissue. I felt bad for him. I also kept my distance. I didn't want to get sick on my trip.

We had only been waiting for a few minutes when the shuttle arrived. Andrew grabbed both of our bags and carried them over. The shuttle bus was less than a quarter full, and there were two seats together near the back.

"You're quiet," he said, after we'd sat.

"I'm a little nervous," I said. "But I'm excited."

"When was the last time you took a vacation?"

"Like a real vacation, out of Utah?" I had to think. "About three and a half years ago. Clive went to New Orleans on business and I went with him."

"I love New Orleans," he said. "Best food in the world."

"I wouldn't know; I only had room service. I never left the hotel."

The shuttle dropped us off at the second terminal. The airport was slammed with pre-Thanksgiving traffic. We walked past most of the travelers to the priority access.

"I'll need your passport," Andrew said as we waited for an agent. I fished it out of my purse and handed it to him. A few minutes later we checked our luggage and got our boarding passes. As Andrew turned from the counter, he said, "If you want, I can keep your passport with mine."

I remembered Carina's paranoid comment about holding my own passport and felt a wave of annoyance. "Thank you. I'd like that."

We still had an hour, so after passing through security, we stopped for coffee, then made our way to the D terminal. When we got to our gate, there was already a large crowd gathered around the entrance to the Jetway. We had been there for only a few minutes when the flight attendant called for boarding for those with premium seating.

"That's us," Andrew said.

"We're in first class?"

He handed me my boarding pass. "Life is too short for economy. You deserve a little pampering." Then he added, "Maybe a lot."

"I don't know if I deserve it, but I like it."

"You deserve it," he said.

I shed my jacket as we walked down the Jet-way.

"Would you like the window or aisle?"

"I don't care."

"I'll let you take the window so you get a good view of Cabo."

The plane was crowded, but I wasn't. The only other time in my life that I had flown first class was seven years ago when Clive was meeting with a client in Pittsburgh, and since it was over a holiday, his client had offered to buy me a ticket as well.

"Did this cost a fortune?" I asked.

"About fifty Christmas trees. But you're worth it."

I settled back in the wide leather chair. "I like the way this trip is starting out."

"Good. It's just the prologue."

I took out my phone. "Here's something else I won't need." I shut it off. "I'm truly unplugged."

A minute later a flight attendant came by to ask if I wanted anything to drink. I ordered a cranberry juice with 7Up, then looked out the window. The snow was still falling and the plane's window was covered with slush.

"We'll probably have to deice the plane," Andrew said.

"How long does that take?"

"It depends on how many planes are ahead of us. Probably about fifteen minutes."

Andrew was right. The plane needed to be deiced. The process sounded like we were going through a car wash. When our plane finally lifted off, Andrew reached over and took my hand, then lay back in his seat. I liked it. I wondered if we would be holding hands on the way back.

CHAPTER
Twenty-One

Cabo is beautiful. My body and soul have
gone from dismal cold to cheerful warm.
> —Maggie Walther's Diary

The flight to Cabo took just under three hours.
Andrew and I talked for most of the first hour
while we ate breakfast. After our trays were
cleared, Andrew read the *Wall Street Journal*
while I reclined my seat and fell asleep. I woke
as we began our descent and the flight attendants
prepared the cabin for landing. Andrew had put a
blanket over me. It made me happy.

I looked out over the blue sea churning with
white foam against the rim of the peninsula. "It's
beautiful," I said. I kissed Andrew on the cheek.

We landed a few minutes later. As I emerged
from the plane, I was surprised by the intensity
of the heat. Even without my coat I was
overdressed. The air was warm and humid and
smelled of flowery perfume. The landscape
around the runways was rugged desert with
the jagged silhouette of mountains rising in the
distance.

We exited the plane from a mobile stairway
attached to the back of a truck, walking carefully

down the rutted metal stairs and onto the hot tarmac below. Andrew paused near the base of the steps and took a deep breath. "It's good to be back."

"When was the last time you were here?" I asked.

"A year ago," he replied.

An airline employee directed us to immigration, which was located in a modern and air-conditioned building, and we claimed our bags. Several other flights had landed about the same time as ours, and there was a lengthy queue.

It took us half an hour to get through immigration. As we walked out into the main terminal, we were mobbed by English-speaking salesmen. Andrew just waved them off, saying, "*No estoy interesado, gracias.*"

"What are you saying?" I asked.

"I told them we're not interested."

"Are they taxi drivers?"

"No, they're selling time-shares."

We picked up our rental car, a cherry-red Mercedes convertible.

"Nice car," I said.

"I thought you'd like it."

"Is the condo far from here?"

"About a half hour. It's a nice drive."

We drove with the top down to the condo at Las Cascadas de Pedregal, a hillside community built along Pedregal beach. We drove past a security guard into a gated complex. The road was dark cobblestone and the grounds were carefully landscaped with exotic desert vegetation. I hadn't been expecting anything this nice.

"This is where we're staying?" I asked.

He nodded. "*Casa, dulce casa.*"

"It's ritzy."

"*Sí.*"

We parked our car in a reserved space in the parking terrace, carried our luggage inside the main building, and took an elevator to the third floor.

Standing in the doorway outside the condo, Andrew said, "It's going to be warm inside. We don't leave the air conditioner on. Electricity is too expensive." Andrew unlocked the door and opened it. There was an immediate loud beeping.

"Sorry, that's the alarm." He stepped over to a panel and dialed a number into it, then flipped on all the room's lights. A half-dozen white enamel ceiling fans began to turn. The far windows were concealed behind drawn drapes.

"Come in," he said. "I'll get the bags."

I stepped inside while Andrew retrieved our luggage. He shut the door and walked to the far side of the room, where he pushed a button on the wall. The drapes parted, revealing a large patio with a panoramic view of the Cabo San Lucas marina and bay.

I literally gasped. "Oh my."

He smiled. "Not bad, right?" He unlocked the glass doors and opened them. "Best view in Cabo."

I walked outside to the edge of the patio. "That is breathtaking."

"You're going to love the sunset," he said. "Then, after its gone, the city lights look like a little galaxy below us. Day or night, there's never a bad view."

The spacious patio had tile floors and a stainless-steel railing along the balcony. Waist-high, brightly colored pots spilled over with equally brilliant bougainvillea. The breeze from the ocean delivered a crisp, briny smell.

It was hard to believe that just six hours earlier I had been shivering beneath dark cloud cover. "What a beautiful day."

"It's always beautiful here," he said, walking up close to me. "That's Medano Beach below us. No SAD here." He looked at me, then added wryly, "Someday we'll find a cure for that."

"I think we just did," I said. I took his hand and looked up at him. "Thank you for bringing me here."

"Thank you for coming." We kissed, then he pulled back, his eyes excited. "Let me show you around."

Holding my hand, he led me back inside. There was an L-shaped suede leather sectional next to a long mahogany dining table.

The kitchen was new and modern, with granite countertops and backsplash and stainless steel appliances. There was original art on the wall— colorful, abstract pieces that chromatically popped from the textured, off-white walls and tan tiled floors.

"I thought we were going to be roughing it," I said. "This is nicer than my home."

"It's a nice little getaway," he said modestly. "They call this area the Beverly Hills of Cabo. The villas around here sell for several million dollars."

"Your friend must be rich," I said. "How long has he owned this?"

"It's been about five years. It was one of the first condos purchased in the development, which is why it has the best views."

"It looks more like five weeks," I said. "It looks brand-new."

"Well, it only gets used a few weeks out of the year, so for all intents, it is." He grabbed my bag. "Your room is back here."

I followed him down a short hallway to a spacious room with a king-sized bed and an ivory-colored, tucked-leather headboard with mahogany trim. He walked to the side of the room and pulled back the drapes, exposing another gorgeous view of the harbor.

"This is the master suite. The bathroom's behind that door right there." He turned on the lights and I walked over and glanced inside. The bathroom was immaculate, with a tile and glass shower and dark cherrywood cabinets. The sinks were two alabaster bowls partially nestled into the counter with gold fixtures. I turned to him. "You should take this room."

"You're my guest," he said.

I walked around the room, then sat on the bed. It was firm but comfortable. I lay back, sinking into the lush padding.

"Passable?" he asked.

I almost laughed. "It's perfect." I sat back up. "Where's your room?"

"It's on the other side of the condo." He looked around. "I need to go to town for groceries. You're welcome to come with me or stay."

"I'll come," I said. "When are we going?"

"No rush. When you're ready. You need time to unpack and freshen up. I'll be out here when you're ready." He walked out of the room. I shut the door behind him, then undressed and got into the shower. I shampooed my hair with a sweet-smelling Mexican shampoo, then sat down on the floor of the shower and let the water wash over me.

Suddenly I began to cry without knowing why. Maybe it was a release, but I hadn't felt this free for as long as I could remember. There was no pain, no shame, no one—besides Andrew—who knew or even cared who I was. I was better than free. I was anonymous. I felt the shame wash off me like the foam running down my body and into the drain.

Best of all, I was with someone who cared about me. *Why did he care about me?* I couldn't remember the last time I had been that happy.

CHAPTER
Twenty-Two

Andrew speaks nearly fluent Spanish. I keep being reminded how false my first perceptions of him were.

—Maggie Walther's Diary

I unpacked all my clothing into the room's empty armoire drawers, then changed into something more appropriate for the Mexican heat—a bright-blue off-the-shoulder romper with a tie at the waist.

I looked at myself in the mirror. It was the first time I had worn the outfit and I thought I looked pretty cute, even if I felt a little self-conscious. Normally I was more conservative in my dress—not that I was prudish; rather, I had just spent too much of my life being noticed by men. But Andrew was different. I wanted him to notice me. I hoped that he would think I looked cute too.

I pulled my hair back over my shoulders and walked back out to the front room. Andrew was sitting on the couch reading a business magazine, and he looked up as I walked in. He stared at me for a moment and said, almost reverently, "*Estás preciosa.*"

I smiled. "*Gracias*. I think." I stepped closer,

then spun a little. "What do you think? You like this?"

"Yes. I especially like you in that."

Andrew had also changed his clothes. He was wearing shorts and had changed his Hawaiian shirt for a short-sleeved white linen shirt. He looked very handsome.

"Sorry I took so long," I said.

"There is no rushing in Cabo," he said. "In fact, I'm pretty sure there's an ordinance against it. I'm reminded of that every time I go into town." He stood. "Shall we go?"

We walked back down to our car and drove about three miles to where the seaside town sat below us. There was a white-sand beach lined with palm trees and saguaro cacti. In the distance, a cruise ship was anchored just outside the harbor. We pulled into the market's parking lot.

MERCADO ORGANICO

Between the two words was a colorful round sign that read:

CALIFORNIA RANCH MARKET
ENJOYING NATURAL AND ORGANIC FOOD

There were several well-used rattan tables and chairs in front of the building with menus on them, which I was glad for, since I hadn't eaten anything since breakfast on the plane. The store was well-stocked and air-conditioned. Most of the product packaging was in English, though there were products I'd never seen before, and the pricing was in both pesos and dollars. We purchased several cases of water, along with fresh fruit: mangoes, peaches, and some strange-looking produce I couldn't identify.

To my surprise, Andrew had a fairly lengthy dialogue in Spanish with the woman at the register ringing up our groceries. She put all our purchases in plastic sacks, and a lanky teenage boy took two of our three bags in his arms.

"How much Spanish do you speak?" I asked Andrew as we walked out of the store.

"Just a little," he said.

"You speak more than a little," I said. "How often do you come down here?"

"Not enough."

"Your friend doesn't use his condo very much?"

He shook his head. "No, he hasn't been here for several years."

"That's a shame," I said.

He nodded slowly. "More than you can imagine."

Andrew opened our car's trunk and the young man, who had followed us out, put the groceries inside. Then he just stood there.

"Does he want something?" I asked.

"Yes; it's different here than in America," Andrew said. "The baggers are volunteers. So we tip them." He took out his wallet and extracted a couple of dollar bills, which he handed to the boy. The boy said *gracias* and ran back to the store.

"They take American dollars?"

"They want American dollars," he said.

We walked back to the store and sat down at one of the tables in front. "I took the liberty of ordering us something to eat," Andrew said.

A few moments later a young woman brought out two fruit drinks in tall, narrow glasses, a bowl of shrimp ceviche, and tortilla chips with a small bowl of guacamole. She said to Andrew, "*Aqui está. Ahorita regreso con su pedido completo.*"

"*Gracias*," he replied.

Andrew handed me a drink.

I looked at him. "What is it?"

"Just try it," he said.

I took a sip. "This is yummy. Mango?"

"Mango and passion fruit." He took a drink from his own glass. "This is good. I didn't know passion fruit was a thing until I came here."

A moment later the young woman returned with a platter of lightly fried rolled tortillas with grated cheese melted on top.

"These are chile and cheese flautas," Andrew said. "You do like Mexican food, I hope."

I laughed. "Do I have a choice?"

"I'm sure we could find a nice Chinese restaurant somewhere."

We shared a caramel flan for dessert.

"I'm going to gain weight here," I said.

"I would hope so."

We went back in the store and picked up the bag of groceries that Andrew had left inside to keep cold, then we drove back to the condominium.

CHAPTER
Twenty-Three

Tonight we ate dinner at a restaurant called Edith's. I was serenaded by a mariachi band. This just keeps getting better.

—Maggie Walther's Diary

Back at the condo, Andrew said, "I need to take care of some business. It might take me a few hours. If you want, there's a swimming pool on the west side of the complex."

"Say no more," I said. "I didn't realize the Christmas tree business required so much tending."

He grinned. "It doesn't. I've got other irons in the fire."

As I started for my room, he said, "We have dinner reservations at six. We should leave around five thirty."

"That gives me four hours to burn."

"Speaking of which, there's sunscreen in your bathroom cabinet."

"That's not what I . . . ." I smiled. "Thank you." I went to my room and changed into a bikini. When I walked out, Andrew was sitting at the couch working on his laptop. He looked up as I entered the room. "Wow."

"Yeah, right," I said. "If pasty white was—"

He held up his hand to stop me. "The proper response is, '*Gracias, Señor.*'"

I smiled. "*Gracias, Señor.*"

"*De nada.* Have fun."

The pool was luxurious and not at all crowded. If this were the antidote to SAD, I could totally overdose on it. The warm fresh air and cool water were emotionally and physically healing. I coated myself in tanning oil and lay out for half an hour before covering up. I was about as white as the snow I'd left behind and didn't want to ruin the trip with a sunburn. I sat under the shade of palm trees and read until four thirty, then went back to get ready for dinner.

When I got back to the condo, Andrew was on his cell phone. He waved at me.

I went to my room and showered, then did my hair and makeup. It was nice to have someone to look nice for. Back when I was married, I would laugh at Carina when she would rate her prospective dates on whether she would shave her legs for them or not. Now that I was single again, I understood that she wasn't joking.

Andrew was waiting for me when I walked back out. "You're going to love this place," he said. "It's called Edith's."

"I had an aunt named Edith."

"Was she Mexican?"

I smiled. "No. She was ornery."

Edith's restaurant was back down on Medano Beach not far from the market where we had shopped earlier. I could see why the restaurant was one of Andrew's favorites. The place looked like a Mexican fiesta. The layout was mostly open—a series of raised, thatched roofs surrounded, at least on the land side, by palm trees and bamboo and thick, snaking vines of bougainvillea.

The thatched roofs were hung with strings of colored glass and punched-tin lanterns and jeweled tin Moravian star pendant lights—the hodgepodge of fixtures hanging above the diners' heads like piñatas. Strings of icicle lights adorned the rim of the fronded canopies. The tablecloths were in bright colors ranging from fuchsia and orange to lime green and scarlet. Around the tables were wicker chairs draped with colorful Mexican blankets.

A trio featuring a violin, a guitar, and an acoustic bass moved throughout the restaurant serenading diners with lively traditional Mexican music, naturally blending in with the overall cacophony.

Adding to the dimmed, noisy atmosphere was a fair amount of fire, not just from the flickering tabletop candle centerpieces and sconces but from long streams of blue liquid fire poured from bottles and silver sauceboats.

"They're big on flambé here," Andrew said. "It's part of the festivities. If it burns, it earns."

"Did you just make that up?" I asked.

"I'm afraid so."

"It was clever."

"It's like the newspaper motto, If it bleeds, it leads."

I frowned. "I've done my share of bleeding in newspapers lately."

"We'll just leave that back in the land of cold," he replied.

Our hostess sat us in a section of the main canopy next to the central kitchen, an open, brick-walled edifice crowded with cooks wearing tall white toques.

"This place is fantastic," I said.

"You haven't tried their food," Andrew replied. "They're famous for their steaks, seafood, and desserts."

I opened the menu and gasped loudly.

Andrew laughed. "You saw the price."

"Shrimp is really seven hundred eighty-five dollars?"

"Pesos," he said.

"But there's a dollar sign."

"They use the same symbol for money. It's confusing, but you can usually figure it out. If it looks outrageously priced, it's pesos."

"How much is a peso worth?"

"Last I checked, about a nickel. So that shrimp dish is about forty dollars."

We decided to order several different plates and share. We had tuna carpaccio and cheese turnovers for appetizers followed by a "flirt" salad, which was made with honey, ginger, and hibiscus liqueur. The presentation of the food was as artistic as our surroundings.

Before we ordered our entrees, our waiter brought out a tray of uncooked meats to exhibit their evening's offerings. We ordered the grilled lobster, shrimp enchiladas, and chile rellenos.

"How long have you been coming here?" I asked.

"Since my first visit to Cabo, about eight years ago. I've eaten here every time since."

"Is Edith a real person?"

Andrew nodded. "She is. I actually met her on my first visit. Her story is amazing. She came to Cabo as a fifteen-year-old girl and got a job here as a waitress. Back then it had a different name, Esmerelda's by the Sea, something like that. Twenty years later she bought out the owner and renamed the restaurant after herself."

"That's a great success story."

"Kind of makes you happy, doesn't it?"

At Andrew's insistence (I didn't provide a whole lot of resistance) we ordered two desserts, the banana flambé and their house flan. While we were eating our dulce, the band made their way to our table.

"What can we play for your lovely lady?" the guitarist asked with a heavy accent.

"How about something romantic," Andrew said.

The guitarist raised his eyebrows. "Ah, you wish romantic. We will play 'Novia Mia.'"

"What does that mean?" I asked Andrew.

"It means my girlfriend," he said.

The trio began playing a lively song with the guitarist belting out the words over the restaurant's din, occasionally accompanied by the slightly out-of-tune, scratchy vocals of the other two band members. After the first stanza, Andrew started laughing.

"What is he saying?" I asked.

"He said, 'Your face is so pretty it will be my torment.'"

The men ended the song with a unified shout, sort of an *olé*! We both clapped. Andrew handed the guitarist a twenty-dollar bill and the men thanked him and moved on to a new table.

"That was fun," I said.

"It's true, you know."

"What's true?"

"Your face has tormented me since I met you."

"That doesn't sound like a compliment."

Andrew started laughing. "Sorry. You're right. Some things don't translate well."

We were in no hurry, so we didn't leave until we'd lingered over our coffees. As we walked into the condo I said, "What a day. It's hard to believe that it began in Utah."

"We're just warming up," Andrew said. "Literally. We've got a full day tomorrow, so we better get some rest."

"What are we doing?" I asked.

"We are going to the sea."

The sea sounded nice. "What time do we leave?"

"We have a boat to catch, so we should leave here by eight thirty."

I glanced down at my watch. "What time is it here?"

"Eleven. Los Cabos is on mountain time, same as home."

I leaned into him. "Good night."

"*Sueños dulces, Linda*. Sweet dreams."

I looked at him. "Did you just call me Linda?"

"*Linda* is Spanish for pretty," he said. "It wasn't a slip."

"Oh good. For a second I thought you were thinking of a previous Cabo guest."

He said, "You're the only woman I've ever brought here. Besides my ex-wife, of course."

"Of course," I echoed. We kissed. After we parted I said softly, "Maybe you could call me something other than Linda. I have an employee named Linda."

"I'll work on it," he said.

We kissed again, this time more passionately.

Our kissing started to physically progress. Then he stepped back. "I need to stop."

"What makes you think I want to stop?" I said.

"It complicates things."

"Oh, that." I sighed. "Good night, handsome."

"Good night, Linda."

I smiled at him, then went to my room and got ready for bed. The blinds were still open, and I could see the city stretched out below me like a rhinestone blanket. I set my watch on the nightstand and climbed into bed. The sheets were fresh and sweet-smelling. I lay back and smiled. I had started the day anxious and cold and ended it happy and warm. I couldn't wait to see what tomorrow would bring.

CHAPTER
Twenty-Four

Something about him makes me throw
caution to the wind. I hope the wind
doesn't return as a tornado.
>   —Maggie Walther's Diary

I woke the next morning bathed in sunlight. It
may have been the same sun as at home, but it
definitely worked a lot harder here.

Andrew was already awake; I could hear him
in the kitchen. I could also smell something
cooking. I got up and put on my swimsuit and
cover up, pulled my hair into a ponytail, then
walked out.

Andrew was standing in front of the stove
frying eggs in a skillet. He wore a blue-and-white
swimsuit, water shoes, and a short-sleeved baby-
blue linen shirt. He looked handsome. He always
looked handsome.

"Good morning, *cariña*," he said.

I sidled up next to him. "Morning." We kissed.
He handed me a cup of coffee. "Thank you," I
said. "*Cariña?*"

"It means cute."

"My best friend's name is Carina, remember?
She works for me too."

"Strike two," he said. "Linda and Carina. Maybe you should give me a list of your employees' names."

"I don't have that many. And I'm pretty sure Kylee and Nichelle aren't Spanish words."

"I'll keep working on it. How did you sleep?"

"Better than usual." I looked at the stove. "What are you making?"

"Huevos rancheros on corn tortillas. Do you like avocados?"

"I love avocados. Almost as much as I love a man who can cook."

"That's good," he said. "Because I am both."

"I have no idea what that means."

"Don't think too much about it." He lifted a fried egg and set it on the crisp tortilla layered with lettuce and refried beans. He dusted it with cilantro, then dropped on some jalapeños. "Those are to wake you up." He handed me the plate.

"I thought you said you didn't cook much."

"Not if I can avoid it," he said.

"You've even got the presentation down."

"I watch cooking shows when I'm bored." He brought over his own plate and a pitcher of guava juice.

"We're off to the sea today?"

"Yes. And beaches. You can only get to the best beaches by boat."

We finished eating and put our dishes in the sink. "Should we clean up?" I asked.

"No, Jazzy will be by to straighten up."

"Jazzy?"

"Sorry. Her real name is Jazmín. She cleans the condo when we're in town."

I went back to my room and got the canvas beach bag I'd brought, along with a book, my iPod, and a few other necessities. When I came back out, Andrew was standing by the door with a large backpack slung over his shoulder. "I've got sunscreen, oil, and towels. There are a few things we need to pick up at the grocery store."

We drove back down to the *mercado* and bought some bread, meat, and cheeses, along with two large bottles of water. We then walked down to the dock to the chartered tour boat, where Andrew was embraced by a short, barrel-chested man with a full beard and mustache and a T-shirt with a picture of David Bowie.

"Maggie, this is my friend, El Capitán."

"Hello," I said, shaking the man's hand. I glanced at Andrew. "You call him the captain?"

"After six years, that's the only name I have for him," Andrew said.

El Capitán gave us each a life jacket and snorkeling equipment, and then his assistant, a thin, ebony-haired teenage girl, gave a brief safety lecture in broken English. We boarded the boat along with three other couples—one Mexican, the other two American.

One of the American couples looked oddly

mismatched. He was in his late fifties, obese and balding with dark sunglasses and a myriad of thick gold chains hanging around his neck and dangling down to his porch of a stomach. The woman was young, probably in her twenties, slim but curvaceous, perfectly tanned, and wearing a revealing string bikini. She had long blond hair, a full sleeve of tattoos on her arm, and massive diamond rings on most of her fingers, which perhaps explained the couple's attraction.

The craft we'd boarded was a long, canopied, glass-bottom boat with smooth, worn wooden benches along its sides. The boat's name was *ABBA*, which was not lost on either of us.

"Your dad would be a fan of this boat," Andrew said, after we'd settled into our seats.

"He would."

"Should I call you Agnetha?"

I grimaced. "No, please. Keep working on it."

Once we had boarded, El Capitán started the outboard engine, the crisp smell of gas and exhaust mixing with brine-scented sea air. The girl untied us from the dock, and we backed out of the slip into the harbor's waterway and headed out to sea.

Our first destination was Pelican Rock, where the boat stopped a hundred yards from shore and dropped floating diving flags. We snorkeled for about half an hour in calm turquoise water teeming with colorful, exotic fish.

The older man didn't leave the boat but his hot little woman did. (Do I sound catty?) I noticed that she swam unnecessarily close to Andrew, occasionally "accidentally" bumping into him. When she wasn't next to him, she looked like she was posing, even provocatively adjusting her swimsuit underwater where anyone with a mask could see. I did my best to focus on the sea life, but the blonde insisted on taking center stage.

After we were back on the boat, Andrew said, "Do you know what the most terrifying sea creature out here is?"

The blonde, I thought. "This sounds like a game show question," I said. "Sharks."

"Hammerhead sharks," the blonde said, inviting herself into our conversation.

"Squids," Andrew said. "Every year, the Humboldt squid comes to the Baja peninsula to feed. The fishermen call them *diablo rojo*, the red devil. They grow as long as nine feet and they've been known to grab people from the surface and pull them under."

"You're making this up," I said.

"Nope. I watched a documentary on it."

"I watch documentaries too," I said. "I saw one on beavers."

Andrew started laughing.

"I'm not kidding. I did."

"I . . ." He shook his head. "So the film crew

sent a cameraman in the water at night wearing a Kevlar jacket."

"What's a Kevlar jacket?" the blonde asked. "Is that like a Gucci jacket?"

I barely suppressed my eye roll.

"It's a bulletproof vest," Andrew said. "And then they waited for the squid to come. The squid have the ability to change their color to match their surroundings, so they're virtually invisible until they're on you."

"Like a stealth squid," the blonde said.

"Exactly," Andrew said. "Only when they're in a feeding frenzy, they flash red and white. The squid attacked the diver and penetrated his vest with its beak."

"Squid have beaks?" I asked.

"Humboldt squid have very sharp beaks. They resemble a parrot's beak, except they're black and the force of their bite is more powerful than an African lion's. They can bite through metal. And their eight tentacles have more than a hundred suction cups, all lined with razor-sharp teeth."

"This is terrifying," the blonde said.

"To make it worse, the Humboldt travel in schools of more than a thousand squid. At night you can see hundreds of tentacles sticking up out of the water, like agave plants."

"What's an agave plant?" the blonde asked.

"It's a succulent," I said, reminding her of my

presence. "With long, sharp, painful spines. You would not want to be stabbed by one." I noticed Andrew grin. "They use it to make tequila."

"I like tequila," she said, moving a little closer to Andrew. "I didn't know they made it from squids."

Andrew didn't bother to explain.

"Is this squid thing real?"

Andrew nodded. "Completely." Then he turned to me and held out his hand. "If my fingers are the legs, the beak is right here," he said, touching the center of his palm. "When they attack, they come at you like this." He put his hand in front of my face.

"This sounds like something you saw in a horror movie," I said.

"Just look at how much you learn being around me," Andrew replied.

"What are you talking about?" the blonde's sugar daddy asked, finally noticing how much attention his woman was giving to Andrew.

"Squids and agave plants," the blonde said.

"Agave," the man said. "That's what they make tequila from."

The blonde leaned toward Andrew. "That thing sounds like a monster."

"It gets worse," Andrew said. "The squid dragged the cameraman down nearly sixty feet before the rope he was tied to broke him free of the squid's grip. The squid was so strong that the diver dislocated his shoulder and his wrist was broken in five places. Had the beast gotten its beak around him, it could have amputated his hand."

"Thank you for not telling me any of this before we snorkeled," I said. "I'm not getting back in the water."

"You don't have to worry. The Humboldt only feed at night."

"That sounds like the name of a horror movie," the blonde said. She pressed her leg against Andrew's. *They Only Feed at Night.*

She's talking about herself, I thought.

Andrew shifted away from her. "And they only live in deep waters," he said to me. "So you don't have to worry about them close to shore."

"I'm still staying on the beach," I said.

From Pelican Rock, our boat sailed to Land's End, the tip of the Baja peninsula, with a pungent ride past a sea lion colony, then on to El Arco de Cabo San Lucas, the famous stone arch.

"Every four years or so, the tide changes enough to create a walkway under the arch," Andrew said.

"Can we walk through it now?" I asked.

"No. Probably next year."

We stopped momentarily at the beach, where El Capitán made an announcement. "Friends, we are now going to Playa del Amor, also called Lovers' Beach. It is very nice sand and calm and good swimming. Next to it is Divorce Beach. It is not so calm, and it has dangerous rip currents. I recommend that you not swim there. Let that be a lesson to you."

Everyone laughed. "I've learned that lesson," I said.

Andrew nodded. "Ditto."

"I will pull the boat up on the shore, and you will exit from the front of the boat. The clock time is nearly eleven. I will be back to get you at the same place I drop you off at four o'clock. Remember, our boat is the *ABBA*. Please do not miss the boat or make your fellow passengers wait for you."

The boat pulled into the beach until its hull was on sand and we made our way out over the bow in single file. I made sure we disembarked after the blonde. I didn't want her following us.

The sand was immaculate, soft and warm, framed by beautiful large rock formations that rose from the sand like sculptures.

Andrew carried our things over to a vacant space about thirty yards from the water, where we laid out our beach towels and rubbed each other down with sunscreen. We spent the next two hours at Lovers' Beach swimming and snorkeling, but as the crowds grew, we moved over toward the less populated Divorce Beach to sunbathe and eat our picnic lunch in privacy. We also ate ripe mangoes and drank passion fruit juice from local vendors. It was a lovely way to spend the day.

Our boat arrived back at Medano Beach as the sun began to set. The blonde and her man were waiting for us on the dock. They invited us up to their villa for drinks, which the woman pointed out on the mountain. Their villa was nearly half as large as the entire complex we were staying at. Andrew thanked them but politely declined their invitation, explaining that we were on our honeymoon.

"Congratulations," the man said. "I hope you remain on Lovers' Beach for as long as you can. Divorce Beach is expensive."

The blonde said nothing but looked at Andrew hungrily.

"Honeymoon?" I said as we walked away.

"I was just trying to refuse them politely," Andrew said.

We ate a simple dinner at a small bar called the Baja Cantina, where we had seafood chowder in sourdough bread bowls, coconut shrimp, and, my favorite, fish tacos.

It was dark when we arrived back at the condo. I was sunburned and tired but happy. The condo was cool and I was glad that the air conditioner had been left on.

I took a quick shower to get the salt and sand off my body, then met Andrew out on the patio. The moon glistened on the water like in a Van Gogh painting. The air was moist and comfortable.

"What's on the agenda for tomorrow?" I asked.

"I thought that after all the travel today, we'd take tomorrow easy. We'll sleep in, do some shopping in town, eat a nice lunch, and then, for after lunch, I made us a reservation at the Spa at Esperanza. It's one of Latin America's top spas."

"This just keeps getting better," I said.

"Even better than Utah?"

"Never heard of the place," I said.

He grinned. "Would you like a strawberry daiquiri?"

"Yes, please."

"I'll be right back."

He stood and walked into the kitchen while I just looked out over the city. About five minutes later he returned carrying two glasses with halved limes on the rims. He handed me one and sat down next to me.

"Thank you," I said. "I keep looking down at the water expecting to see a bunch of squid legs sticking out."

He laughed. "They're tentacles, not legs. And I'm sorry I told you about them. I didn't mean to ruin the water for you."

"Was that all true?"

"Every word of it."

"That blonde would have liked to pull you under."

He looked at me with an amused grin. "She was just being friendly."

I took a drink of my daiquiri, then said, "Yeah, right. If we'd been there much longer, she would have ended up in your lap. I wanted to clock her."

"I'm glad you didn't," Andrew said. "I think that guy she was with was in the Mafia." He took a small sip of his drink and set it down. "I like seeing you jealous."

"I'm not jealous," I said, sounding like a liar even to myself. "Maybe a little."

He lifted his drink. "You should try this. It's virgin."

"You're drinking a virgin daiquiri?"

He nodded.

"I noticed that you don't drink much."

"I used to. Especially whenever things went bad." He looked at me dolefully. "Back then, a lot of things were going bad."

"What kind of things?"

"Marriage. Family. Business. Pretty much everything that mattered."

"I'm sorry," I said. "But today was a perfect day. Thank you again for talking me into coming here."

"I knew it would be good for you to be here," he said. "And me."

"You know me," I said.

"I'd like to."

I looked out over the bay, then closed my eyes,

feeling the warm wind pressing against my face, brushing back my hair. I breathed it in and felt right with the world. After a few more minutes of silence I said, "It's been a long time since I've felt like this."

"How is that?"

"Happy." I looked into his eyes. Then the words came out. "In love."

He just looked at me. I suddenly felt awkward. "I'm sorry. I—"

"I feel the same," he said. "You just beat me to it."

His words sounded like joy. I set down my drink and nestled into him. We stayed that way for nearly an hour. Finally I said, "I'm tired. I guess I'll go to bed."

He kissed me on the forehead. "I'm going to sit out here a little longer. Good night."

"Night," I said.

We kissed and I got up and went to my room. As I lay in bed I couldn't believe that I had told him that I loved him. I hoped it wouldn't ruin our trip.

CHAPTER
Twenty-Five

When I first met Andrew, I took him for an attractive, simple man selling Christmas trees to keep the lights on. Not the case. He's attractive, but he's also smart, cosmopolitan, and possibly rich. He not only provided my plane ticket and accommodations, he's also paying for all my meals and activities. Today we went to the Spa at Esperanza. (I think I spelled that right.) It was a day of perfect pampering. It was the perfect everything.

—Maggie Walther's Diary

In spite of Andrew's invitation to sleep in, I woke early. Andrew must have been exhausted because I peeked into his room and he was sprawled out on top of his covers asleep and lightly snoring.

I put on my walking shorts and a tank top and went out walking, first around the complex, then all the way down to the edge of the beach and back. I passed a cactus garden with more than thirty different varieties of cacti. I had never realized how beautiful cacti were. I had just always thought of them as something painful to avoid. Maybe there's a metaphor there.

When I got back to the condo, Andrew was sitting outside on the patio drinking coffee.

He smiled when he saw me. "Where'd you go?"

"Just on a walk," I said. "I walked down to the beach and back."

"I was afraid you ran off with someone else."

I walked over, sat on his lap, and kissed him. "I like seeing you jealous too."

A half hour later we drove downtown and parked just a little east of the *mercado*. The area was crowded with tourists patronizing the area's street vendors, clothing shops, and restaurants. After we had walked around a while, we went to the flea market, which covered several acres and was filled with vendors hawking pottery, clothing, cheap jewelry, electronic gadgets, and all the usual touristy knickknacks. I didn't buy anything except a shaved ice and a hat, as the sun was frying me.

After the flea market we walked over by the marina and found a place to sit beneath the shade of a palm tree.

"There are so many boats," I said.

"I counted them all once," Andrew said. "Not that it means anything, since the number changes hourly. There were a hundred and forty-seven."

"What prompted you to count them?"

"My OCD. I'm always counting things. Maybe that's why I got into finance."

"Have you ever sailed?"

"I used to," he said. "A lot. Back when I had a boat."

"You owned a boat?"

He nodded, his expression looking slightly nostalgic. "A thirty-five footer. I called her *A Meeting*."

"A Meeting?"

"That way, when I was out playing and my clients called, my secretary could say, 'He's in *A Meeting* right now.'"

I grinned. "Brilliant."

"I loved that boat. I had to sell her when the business went down." He sighed. "I still dream of retiring in a little place on the sea with a fishing boat, just big enough to go in deep waters. Something about the size of Hemingway's boat."

"Hemingway the author?"

Andrew nodded. "Hemingway loved the sea. He had a thirty-eight-foot fishing boat called the *Pilar*, after his second wife's nickname. He was an avid, if unconventional, fisherman. They said that he took a tommy gun with him on his boat to shoot sharks if they tried to feed on his catch.

"Once he and a friend caught a thousand-pound marlin, the largest either of them had ever caught. As they tried to bring it in, sharks came after it. Hemingway got out his tommy gun and started blasting them, but his plan backfired. The shooting created so much blood and chum in the water that it drew hundreds of sharks in a feeding frenzy. They ended up with only half their prized catch.

"It ruined the men's friendship, since Hemingway's friend blamed his use of the gun for the loss of the biggest fish he'd ever caught. On the bright side, the world benefited, as it became the impetus for his book *The Old Man and the Sea.*"

"You are a surprising font of knowledge," I said.

"I read a lot," he said.

"I've always wondered what it is about men and boats."

"I've wondered too," he said. "Maybe we're just naturally wired with wanderlust, and the sea is our last viable frontier."

"Do you have wanderlust?"

He didn't look at me. "Sometimes I dream of disappearing," he said softly.

I looked back out over the marina. "My father's boat looked kind of like that one." I pointed to a sleek, twenty-plus-foot vessel in a slip across from us. "At least that's how I remember it. I only saw it once."

"Why is that?"

"It wasn't for us. He bought it with the insurance settlement after my mother died. I didn't see much of him after that."

For the next half hour we just watched the boats cruise in and out of the marina.

"Look at the size of that yacht right there," I said. "I wonder how much it cost."

"Probably a couple million," Andrew said. "There's money here." He pointed to a boat idling about a hundred yards from the dock. "See that yacht out there?"

"The one with sails or the huge black-and-gold one next to it?"

"The black-and-gold one next to it. My friend used to own it."

"It's giant. Your same friend who owns the condo?"

He nodded. "It's beautiful inside. I wish I could show it to you. It has marble countertops, hardwood floors, a formal dining room. It even has a dance floor."

"How much does a boat like that cost?"

Andrew smiled. "If you have to ask, you can't afford it."

"I already know I can't afford it."

"A little over three million."

"Your friend is very rich."

"He was," Andrew said. "Now he's just rich." He looked back out at the boat. "They changed its name. It used to be called *Seas the Day*."

"Carpe diem," I said.

"Except he spelled *seize* s-e-a-s."

"That's clever."

"He liked word plays. It was either that or *Nauti Buoy, naughty* spelled like *nautical, buoy* like an ocean *buoy*."

"Was he?"

"Was he what?"

"A naughty boy?"

"He was back then. Not so much these days."

"I'd like to meet him."

He turned to me. "I don't think I want you to meet him."

"Why is that?"

"He would like you."

I kissed him on the cheek. "You have nothing to worry about."

We ate lunch at a small seafood restaurant and pub on the marina, then walked around until it was time for our spa appointment.

The Spa at Esperanza lived up to its billing. After checking in, we spent the first half hour in their signature therapy pool, the Pasaje de Agua, for a water-passage purifying ritual, which basically involved moving back and forth from warm to cool water. We started in a warm-spring soaking pool, moved to the steam cave, then out to a cool waterfall rinse.

Afterward we donned thick terry-cloth bathrobes and sat in a quiet room until two therapists came for us. Andrew had booked us a treatment called "Romancing the Stone," which consisted of a deep heat stone massage followed by a private soaking tub, then scalp and foot massage. The whole treatment lasted three hours and I don't remember the last time that I felt so spoiled or relaxed. All my muscles felt like soft rubber.

As we exited the spa, I noticed the price tag on our treatment was nearly a thousand dollars each.

"What did you think of that?" Andrew asked as we walked out.

I sighed happily. "I think I just went to heaven."

"Glad to take you there," he said.

We ate dinner close to our condo at a restaurant called El Farallón at the Resort at Pedregal.

"What does *el Farallón* mean?" I asked.

"*Farallón* is a rocky outcrop."

The restaurant was built on a platform of rock jutting from the hillside. "Hence the name."

"Hence the name," he said.

I ordered carrot and coconut-milk soup with curry and goat cheese, then we shared a lobster ceviche with grilled pineapple. For dinner I had sea bass with saffron rice and bell peppers, and grilled corn with epazote mayonnaise. For dessert we shared a tres leches cake with raspberries.

As in most Latin American restaurants, no one was in a hurry, so we ate and talked and laughed until past ten. I drank a little too much wine, so after dinner Andrew had to help me to the car, then up to our condo and my bed. I sat down on the bed and lifted my feet. "Please take off my shoes."

He knelt down and took them off. "Your feet are free," he said. He stood and sat on the bed next to me.

I leaned into him. "This has been the best day ever."

"At least until tomorrow," Andrew said.

"What are we doing tomorrow?"

"What would you like to do tomorrow?"

I touched my finger to his face, tracing the edge of his stubbled chin. "Be with you."

"That's a given. I was thinking that we might go for a drive to Todos Santos. It's a Mexican hamlet about an hour north of us. I think you'll like it. It has a unique charm."

"If all I wanted was a unique charm, I could just stay here with you."

"And they have great fish tacos," he said.

I couldn't believe how in love I was.

CHAPTER
Twenty-Six

Today we visited a lovely, quaint little town about an hour north called Todos Santos. Andrew took me to a remote beachfront house he's seriously considering buying to escape to. I would like someplace to escape to. Or maybe just some*one*.

—Maggie Walther's Diary

We ate a quick breakfast of coffee and black sapote—an indigenous fruit that tastes like chocolate pudding—and baked breakfast rolls stuffed with ham, cheese, and chipotle.

We packed our swimsuits and towels, got in our car, and drove north to Pueblo Mágico Todos Santos. The Pueblo Mágico (Magic Town) title had been added a decade earlier by Mexico's Tourism Secretary to recognize it as a colonial town with historical relevance.

Andrew gave me a rundown of the town's history as we drove. Todos Santos was founded in the seventeen hundreds by Jesuit missionaries who came to establish a farming community with the intent of providing food for the nearby city of La Paz. The success of the community led to the founding of the Santa Rosa de las Palmas mission. Later, as its population grew, the town became a major sugarcane producer. It was also the site of the last battle of the Mexican-American War.

We drove north along Highway 19, a narrow, winding desert road that runs along the Pacific coast of Baja California Sur. The drive was pretty, with desert landscape, Joshua trees, and brightly colored flowers and cactus. There wasn't much traffic and Andrew and I talked the whole way.

"Todos has a town motto," Andrew said to me as the town came into view. " 'Nothing bad ever happens here.'"

"I definitely should move here," I said.

"I'm seriously considering it," he said. "In the last few decades it's become an artist colony. Artists, writers, and musicians come here from all over. It's a little bit ironic: they came here because it was cheap and private, then their coming drew the public, making it not so cheap and private." He looked at me. "The tortured life of an artist."

"Are you an artist?" I asked.

"People used to say I was an artist with money," he said. "But what I really wanted to be was a novelist. That was the dream."

"What happened to your dream?"

"It got woken by the cold plunge of reality."

He looked at me. "What about you? Any artistic pursuits outside the kitchen?"

"I've painted some."

"Are you good?"

"Do I still have a day job?"

His brow furrowed. "I don't know."

"You sound like Carina." As we drove into town, I said, "Deep inside, do you still have that dream of writing?"

He looked reflective. "I think I have stories to tell." He looked at me and smiled. "I don't know if anyone will want to read them, but I have them."

"I'll read them," I said.

"Good. I'll tell the publishers I have a reader."

The town of Todos Santos was old and picturesque. The mission church reminded me a little of the Alamo, at least the pictures I'd seen of it, and the cobblestone streets were overhung by colorful flags draped from the buildings that lined them.

The small town, like most tourist attractions, had an inordinate number of restaurants. Andrew called it a "foodie mecca," which was good because this week I was unleashing my inner foodie. I was definitely going to gain weight.

"One of the best places for lunch is a food truck run by two women friends," he told me as we walked toward town. "A few years ago *Condé Nast Traveler* did an article on them that made them world famous. One of the owners is a well-known Mexican actress and the other is a chef. They claim that their truck always has the freshest fish in town because the local fishermen are smitten with the women's beauty."

"We definitely need to eat there," I said.

"I've never been disappointed."

"With the food or the women?"

He smiled. "Either."

We found the food truck parked near the main park. It was fittingly called La Chulita, which in Mexican slang roughly translates to "li'l sexy mama." One of the famed women was there, Daphne. She was pretty and dressed in retro clothing, her dark hair pinned up in a fifties-style hairdo. The truck specialized in ceviche; some claim it's the best in Mexico. We ordered two kinds: the first with clams, scallops, and marlin with corn, poblano chilies, and avocado; and the second with shrimp, mango, and pineapple. Both were excellent.

We spent the afternoon walking along the town's main thoroughfare, stopping in three different art galleries and two different bakeries.

"How did you find this place?" I asked, eating a sweet cream-cheese pastry.

"I read about it in a travel book," he said. "It was my third or fourth visit to Cabo. Sometimes the resort life gets a little staid. I came here by motorcycle."

"That sounds adventurous."

"Driving in Mexico is always adventurous," he said. "But back then, I was just trying to be a rebel."

"Were you?"

"Still am," he said. "I just need a cause."

Andrew continued to tell me about the places we walked by, usually in remarkable detail. Finally, I asked, "How do you know so much about this place?"

"I've thought about moving here."

"You were serious, then. About your dream of retiring on the sea?"

He nodded. "There's a little hacienda on the beach just south of town. It even comes with a fishing boat. I've thought of buying it."

"With your Christmas tree profits."

He smiled. "Exactly."

"But if you bought it, you'd be down here—"

"That's the general idea."

"And I'd be up there. In the snow."

His brow furrowed. "That would be a problem." He looked at me. "But not one that would be hard to remedy."

I didn't know what to say to that. "I'd like to see your dream place."

"I'll take you by it on the way home."

We just wandered around the town until late afternoon, then Andrew took me to see the hacienda. There was nothing around it for miles.

It was a charming little cottage painted coral pink with a large back porch for sitting and watching the sea. It was still for sale. The boat was gone.

"She must be out to sea," Andrew said.

"Who?" I asked.

"The boat. She's called *El Sueño*."

"What does that mean?"

He smiled. "The dream."

We started our journey back to Cabo with a side trip to Cerritos Beach, about ten miles south of Todos Santos. The road to Cerritos was a little rugged and a lot bumpy. Fortunately, Andrew not only knew the way but assured me that it was worth the rough ride.

It was. The beach was spectacular, and maybe it was the hour, but it wasn't crowded like any of the other beaches we'd been to. There were only a few local surfers and some fishing boats in the distance.

"I think that's her," Andrew said, pointing out to the horizon. "*El Sueño*."

I changed into my bathing suit in the car and we went out for a swim. As the sun touched the horizon, Andrew laid out a towel and we sat on the beach and watched the sun set. For more than fifteen minutes neither of us spoke. It was too serene to ruin with words. When the sun was half drowned, Andrew put his arm around me. "I could do this every night. It never gets old."

Me too, I thought.

"It's Thanksgiving tomorrow," he said.

In the crush of our activity, I'd actually forgotten. "Do they celebrate Thanksgiving in Mexico?"

"Some do. It's a US holiday, but it's becoming more popular."

"Do we have plans?" I asked.

"I always have a plan," he said. "Not always a good one, but at least it's a plan."

"Are you going to tell me about it?"

"No."

I lay back onto his lap. "Okay."

We stayed nearly an hour after the sun was gone. We got back to the condo at around midnight and went straight to bed.

CHAPTER
Twenty-Seven

I've heard many people speak about putting the "thanks" in Thankgiving, but today, Andrew showed me how to put in the "giving."

—Maggie Walther's Diary

"Good morning," Andrew said, pulling up the blinds in my room.

I opened my eyes to see him standing next to my bed, silhouetted by the morning sun.

"Good morning. What time is it?"

"Almost ten. I thought I'd better wake you." He walked over to the table and lifted a tray. "I brought you breakfast."

"You brought me breakfast in bed?"

"I'm sorry; you can have it in the kitchen if you like. Or on the patio."

"Don't apologize," I said, laughing. "No one's ever brought me breakfast in bed."

"It sounds great," he said, "but the truth is, it's hard to eat. I mean, you can't really move around, and you're worried about spilling your juice and coffee the whole time."

"That's what Clive always said. It was his excuse for not ever doing it."

Andrew had brought me a bowl of yogurt with raspberries and blueberries, sliced melon, and a unique pastry I'd never seen before. "What's this?"

"It's a *concha*," he said. "That's Spanish for seashell."

"It looks like a seashell."

"It's very popular here. It's like a cookie baked on top of cinnamon bread."

I took a bite. Not surprisingly, it was delicious.

"Happy Thanksgiving," he said.

"Happy Thanksgiving. You said we have plans?"

"I have a Thanksgiving tradition. I hope you don't mind me commandeering the day."

"You've commandeered every day since we got here," I said. "I'm not complaining."

"Good. Then as soon as you're ready, we'll go."

"Where are we going?"

"*A bendecir vidas*," he said, then walked out of the room.

I took a quick shower and dressed, then walked out to the kitchen. Andrew was on the couch reading a thriller.

"Let's go," he said.

"Where to?" I asked again. "In English this time, *por favor*."

"Back to the *mercado*."

"We're shopping for Thanksgiving?"

"Yes, we are."

"We should make a list," I said.

"I already have."

As we walked inside the *mercado*, the woman Andrew had spoken with on our first day embraced him. He followed her over to the register and she handed him a piece of paper that had handwriting on both sides. He examined the paper and then gave her a credit card, which I thought was curious, since we hadn't purchased anything yet.

After he signed the bill, she handed him a set of keys. Andrew turned to me. "We're done here."

"But we didn't buy anything yet."

"They took care of everything."

We walked out of the store. Instead of walking to our car, Andrew walked toward a small delivery truck with the name of the *mercado* printed on the side.

"We've changed vehicles," he said. "Hop in."

"We're taking a truck?"

"We need the space," he said. "And where we're going, the car would be an insult."

"Where are we going?"

A large smile crossed his face. "We're delivering Thanksgiving."

"To who?"

He held up the sheet of paper that the woman at the *mercado* had given him. "To the list."

We drove east, passing from the lush, gated

communities and manicured yards of the tourist side of Los Cabos into a poor area of town, revealed in steadily declining buildings and neighborhoods.

The poor section of Los Cabos was only a few miles from the yachts, golf courses, and luxury resorts, but a universe away for the locals.

"This is San José del Cabo," Andrew said.

I looked around at the graffiti-strewn walls and abandoned buildings. It looked like a war zone. "Is it safe?"

"It's safe for us," he said. "The gangs usually leave American tourists alone. But especially us."

"The gangs know you?"

"It took a few years," he said.

He pulled the truck into a neighborhood that had all the makings of a refugee camp. Dozens of poles stuck up from the ground with electric cables crisscrossing in a nest of wires.

"When they built the resorts, no one took time to plan out where the workers would live, so these communities sprouted up." He turned off the truck. "This is what a town looks like without urban planning." He opened his door. "Come on."

I met Andrew at the back of the truck as he opened the cargo doors. The truck was stacked nearly to the top with boxes, dozens of them. He pulled out a box that was smaller than the rest. "I'll have you take that. It's for the children."

I looked inside the box. It was filled with Hershey's chocolate bars. Andrew grabbed one of the large boxes, then shut the doors.

As we walked to the first home, the door opened and a woman holding a baby emerged. "*Señor Colina, me da gusto a verle. Pásele por favor.*" She held the door open for us.

"She invited us in," Andrew said.

We walked inside. The home had dusty concrete floors and painted plastered walls, though the paint had mostly faded and much of the plaster had flaked off. On one side of the house was a kitchen and dining area with an old wooden table and a cupboard next to it. A wooden pallet fastened to the wall held aluminum pans hung from twisted, rusted wires. A blanket hung on the other side of the room as a partition, giving a scrap of privacy to the bedroom behind it, which had a single wide bed raised off the floor on cinderblocks. A naked lightbulb hung from the center of the room, its wires exposed.

In contrast to the concrete and plaster were colorful woven blankets and pictures hanging on the walls, bringing a sort of chromatic brilliance to the dusty room. The largest picture was an image of the Virgin Mary positioned next to a wooden cross icon with a crucified Jesus.

At the side of the room two dirty-faced children sat on a faded red couch next to a young girl who was nursing a baby. She looked too young to be a mother. The children's eyes were wide with excitement, and they sprang from the couch when they saw us.

Andrew set the box of food on the table, saying to the woman, "*¿Cómo está, Señora Abreyta?*"

"*Estamos bien. Mi hija ha regresado a vivir conmigo. Esta es su hija.*"

"*¿Ella es su nieta?*"

"*Sí.*"

"*Ella se parece a usted.*" Andrew said to me, "This is her granddaughter."

"*Bella,*" I said.

She smiled, then said in a thick accent, "Thank you."

The children were now standing in front of us, staring at the box I held.

"They remember that box from last year," Andrew said. "You can give them some chocolate."

I reached into the box and handed them each a chocolate bar. It might as well have been gold bullion for the excitement on their faces.

"*¡Gracias!*" they shouted. They ran back to the couch and peeled open their treats.

"*Que Dios le bendiga, Señor.*"

"*Ya lo hizo.*"

The woman kissed Andrew on the cheek, then she kissed me as well. "*Por favor comen con nosotros.*"

"*Gracias,*" Andrew said, "*pero no podemos.*

Tenemos que visitar a otros." He turned to me. "She's asking us to stay. They all will. We should go."

"*Cuidense mucho,*" he said to her and the rest of the family.

"*Adiós,*" I said.

I preceded him out, carrying the box of candy. As soon as I got in the truck, I began to cry.

Andrew climbed in the other side of the truck, buckled himself in, and looked over at me. "Are you okay?"

I turned back to him. "I can't believe I've felt so sorry for myself."

"One Thanksgiving I realized that the day had become meaningless to me. I was ungrateful and unhappy. That's when I realized that I was unhappy *because* I was ungrateful. That's when I started doing this. It benefits me more than them."

"How many years have you done this?"

"Six," he said. "A few years ago I missed a year. It's probably when I needed it the most." He marked the first name off the paper using a stub of a pencil. "One down."

"How did you get your list of people?"

"Rosa at the *mercado* helped me. When I first started, I asked her to put together a list of people who could use some help. The first year there were only three families."

"Your list has grown."

Andrew grinned. "Word gets out. It's hard to say no."

Andrew put the truck in gear and we drove just a few blocks to the next home. We spent the next two hours visiting homes, slowly depleting our truck of its contents. The homes were all different but, in one way, the same—humble, makeshift structures cobbled together with whatever materials their inhabitants could scavenge or afford at the time. As Andrew had predicted, every one of the families invited us to stay and eat with them, which Andrew politely declined.

As we neared the end of our deliveries, Andrew pulled the van into the middle of an open dirt lot. We were immediately surrounded by a group of tattooed, rough-looking youths. To my surprise, Andrew turned off the engine. He glanced over at me and said, "Don't be afraid. We're okay," then got out.

One of the larger and older youths approached him. To my surprise, he and Andrew embraced. Then, followed by the others, they walked around to the back of the truck. Soon several of the men walked past me, each carrying a box, going his own way. About five minutes later Andrew opened the driver's door. "That's the last of it."

"We're done?"

"Not quite," he said. He looked at me. "Are you okay?"

"Yeah. That just scared me a little."

193

"I wouldn't have put you in danger." He started up the truck. "We're going to have dinner with one of the families we left food with. It was the fourth home we stopped at. The Villaltas."

Andrew drove back to one of the neighborhoods where we'd started our distribution. We stopped in front of a house we'd already been to. Before we could get out of the truck, a short Mexican man emerged from the house. "*Bienvenido, amigo.*"

Andrew quickly got out. "*Señor Villalta, regresamos.*"

"*Señor Colina, mi amigo, mucho gusto a verle de nuevo.*" The men embraced. Then he looked at me. "*Tiene una compañera. ¿Es su esposa?*"

"*No. Solo una amiga.*"

As I got out of the truck, the man said to me. "*¿Habla español?*"

I turned to Andrew. "He wants to know if I speak Spanish?"

Andrew nodded. "*Un poco,*" he said to the man, which was a gross overstatement of my lingual abilities.

"Welcome, *Señorita,*" he said in a thick accent. "My name *es* Ed-ward."

"It's nice to meet you," I said slowly.

He turned to Andrew and raised his eyebrows. "*Ella es muy bonita.*"

Andrew nodded. "*Sí, ella es muy bonita.*"

I understood that.

"Maggie," Andrew said, "there's a paper bag behind your seat, would you grab it?"

"*Sí, Señor*," I said, trying to be funny.

"*¡Mira! Habla español!*" the man said.

I grabbed the sack. It was heavy with a bottle inside. I followed the men into the house.

The inside of the home was slightly larger, though more narrow, than the first home we'd visited. The walls had also once been plastered and painted but the plaster had mostly chipped off, revealing the concrete walls underneath. Electrical wires hung along two of the walls, which they used to hang pictures, mostly older, photographic portraits of relatives and one large, colored poster of the pope. There was a rusted metal floor fan on the far side of the room next to one of the home's two clouded windows.

The main room's furniture consisted of a pair of couches set side by side and covered with bright blankets. I could see the two boxes of food we'd left earlier in the kitchen area, which was higher ceilinged than the rest of the house and had an exposed pitched roof of corrugated tin. It looked to be an addition to the house, as the plaster walls gave way to bare cinderblock.

Noticeably, they had an oven and a refrigerator. Both were smaller than anything I'd seen in the US, but a rare luxury among the houses we had visited. The smell of a baking turkey and ham filled the small room.

"Mag, I'll take that," Andrew said, reaching for the sack I held. I handed it to him.

"*¿Dondé está la Señora Villalta?*"Andrew asked.

"*Se fue a la tienda para comprarles un refresco.*"

"*Ustedes son muy amables. Muchas gracias, amigo.*"

Andrew turned to me. "I asked him where his wife was. He said she went to the store to get us sodas."

"She didn't need to do that," I said.

"It's important to them that they be good hosts." Andrew turned back to the man. "Then I can give this to you." Andrew slowly pulled an oval-shaped bottle of clear liquor from the sack.

The man looked at it in awe. "*¡Señor es un milagro! Muchísimas gracias!*"

"*De nada,*" Andrew said.

I smiled to see how happy the gift made our host. "What is that?"

"It's called sotol. It's a special liquor made from a desert plant like tequila, but it's especially potent. They say the first glass sharpens the senses, the second the conscience." Andrew handed the bottle to the man, who took it reverently. "It takes more than twelve years to mature, so it's expensive."

"How did you know he liked it?"

"When I first met him, he asked me if I had

ever tried it. I had never even heard of it. He told me that it was the *néctar de los dioses*. Nectar of the Gods. He said that as a young man he had tried it once. He spoke of it like it was a lost love. I thought I'd make his dream come true."

Andrew turned back to the man. "*¿Y como está la familia?*"

I didn't know what Andrew had said, but the man's disposition abruptly changed. "*Estos son tiempos difíciles, amigo.*"

"He said their family is going through a difficult time," Andrew said. "*¿Que pasó?*"

The man's face showed still more pain. "*Ángel se unió con una pandilla. Le dieron una coche y dinero. Le mataron por una pistola después de nueve días.*" He pointed toward the door. "*Hace dos semanas que su hermana lo encontró tres calles por allá.*"

Andrew embraced the man and said, "*Mis condolencias.*"

I didn't know what was said, but tears fell down the man's cheeks. Andrew turned to me. To my surprise, his eyes were also wet. "A month ago their son joined a drug gang. He was killed nine days later. His sister found his body."

I looked at the man. "I am so sorry." I walked over and hugged him.

"*Gracias, Señora.*"

He wiped his eyes with his sleeves, then said, "*No quitaré más de su visita. Estoy agradecido.*"

197

A few minutes later Mrs. Villalta returned escorted by two teenage girls. She was carrying bottles of Jarritos soda. She was about the same build as her husband, short and broad, though lighter of complexion. The girls looked to be in their early teens.

"*Señor Colina*," she said, "*nos dió tanto este año.*"

"*¿Todavía está bien a cenar con usted?*" Andrew asked.

"*¡Sí! ¡Sí! Estamos listos!*"

"She said, 'Let's eat.'"

Their table was set with the food we'd brought, as well as fresh tortillas and tamales. Their utensils were mismatched and the plates were small, battered aluminum pizza tins.

"Edward found these tins in a Dumpster behind a pizzeria where he was weeding," Andrew said to me. "Before that we used pieces of cardboard."

As we were sitting down, I asked, "Why does everyone call you Mr. Colina?"

"*Colina* means hill," Andrew said. "My last name."

"*Nuestro hogar es humilde*," the man said to us.

"*No, no. Es un honor para nosotros*," Andrew said. "He just told us his house is humble."

"*Oraremos*," Mrs. Villalta said. She turned to me and said in English, "We pray."

I didn't understand anything she said, but she offered a lengthy and impassioned prayer and began crying just a few minutes in. After saying "Amen," everyone in the family crossed themselves and began to eat.

The turkey we'd brought them was large and would last them for several meals, which I wanted them to have, so in spite of our hosts' constant entreaties, I ate only a little.

"*Coma, coma,*" Mrs. Villalta said. "*Está delgada.*" She turned to Andrew to translate.

"She's telling you to eat," Andrew said. "She says you're too skinny."

"Tell her thank you," I said.

Andrew looked at me. "She didn't mean it as a compliment."

For dessert we had sweet cinnamon tamales wrapped in corn husks. It was several hours before we left their home, the Villaltas doing all they could to extend our stay. As we drove away, I asked, "Why did she start crying during the prayer?"

"She was praying for her son's soul," Andrew said.

"I was sorry to hear about their son."

Andrew exhaled heavily. "It's a tragedy. The poverty is especially hard on them in Cabo. Poverty is hard anywhere, but here they can see the resorts and the wealthy foreigners' boats and cars, so they know what they're missing. Then they see the wealthy Mexican drug traffickers, and it seems like selling drugs is the only way out for them. It's especially sad, as I had just gotten Edward a good gardening job at the condominiums and things were looking up for their family. The young woman who cleans our place, Jazmín, is his niece."

We returned the truck to the *mercado*, then took a walk along the beach. I again took off my shoes. It would be my last chance to walk barefoot in the sand before returning to Utah. I felt sad at that thought. After a while Andrew turned to me. "I hope it was okay that we spent our Thanksgiving that way. I should have told you what I was up to."

"It was a privilege," I said. "I don't think I'll ever forget it."

"Hopefully it won't be your last time," he said.

I looked at him and smiled. "Hopefully."

"But it is exhausting."

"I was just thinking that I could use a nap," I said. "It's the tryptophan in the turkey. It's like a sleeping drug."

"I don't think you consumed enough of it to affect you," he said. "But I could use a nap."

We drove back to the condo. As we walked in, Andrew said, "Would you like to take a nap with me?"

"Yes."

I followed him into his room. It was the first time I'd actually been in it. It was not as large as mine but it was also nicely furnished, decorated with framed Mexican landscapes on the walls.

Andrew noticed me looking at them. "I bought those in Todos Santos."

"That's nice of you to buy art for your friend's condo," I said.

He smiled. "Least I could do."

I slipped off to my own room to brush my teeth and use the bathroom. When I came back, Andrew was lying on top of the sheets on the bed. I knelt on the side of the bed and crawled over to him, cuddling up against his chest. Without a word, he wrapped his arms around me, his chin against the crown of my head. I fell asleep to the sound of his heart beating.

CHAPTER
Twenty-Eight

Have I ever been so in love? Has my heart
ever been in such peril?
— Maggie Walther's Diary

We slept until nearly six p.m. At least, I did.
Andrew was already up. He woke me, gently
shaking me. "We need to go in ten minutes," he
whispered.

I rolled over. "Go?"

"We have dinner reservations."

I sat up, covering my mouth to yawn. "Where
are we going?"

"I'm taking you to one of my favorite restaurants. It's called Sunset Mona Lisa."

"That sounds romantic."

"It's the perfect place to end our vacation."

End. The word sent a twinge of sadness through
my heart. I never wanted this to end.

The restaurant, Sunset Mona Lisa, wasn't
far from our condominium. We left our car
with the valet and walked inside the building
to check in, though the dining area was almost
entirely outdoors—a series of terraced patios
with wood-planked or tile inlaid floors, built

around sapphire-blue pools and white-linen-draped tables and fire pits.

"You don't just walk into this restaurant," Andrew said, as we entered. "It's very popular. I booked it the same night you said you'd go. Luckily there was one last opening for two."

"So you had this up your sleeve the whole time."

"I don't like to leave things to chance."

The restaurant's maître d', a tall, handsome Mexican man, led us to our table near the edge of the lowest terrace. Our view overlooked the shore and the Pacific Ocean, which was now retreating with the sun.

Andrew tipped the man, then sat back in his chair looking very pleased. A pretty, older Mexican woman brought us our menus. "*Buenas tardes.*"

"*Buenas tardes,*" Andrew repeated. "*¿Qué tal?*"

"*Muy bien.*" She looked at me, then said in clear English, "What may I bring you to drink?"

Andrew said to me, "May I order something for you?"

"Yes. Please."

"Please bring us each a glass of Dom Pérignon 2004."

"*Muy bien.* Are you ready to order?"

"We're still looking over our menus. In the

meantime, would you bring us the calamari appetizer and the carpaccio?"

"*Sí.*"

"Dom Pérignon?" I said after the woman left. "Champagne?"

"We're celebrating."

I smiled at him. "What are we celebrating?"

He pointed toward the west. "The sun. And you being in remission from SAD."

I gazed out over the horizon. "But our sun is leaving us."

"She'll be back tomorrow."

"And then we'll be leaving." I sighed. "I wonder what the weather's like at home."

"I'd rather not talk about going home yet."

"I'm sorry. What should we talk about?"

"How about the moment?" he said.

"We should toast that," I said. "It's a much better toast than loneliness."

"Or your car," Andrew added. He looked around. "This is considered one of the coolest restaurants in the world. I think the *New York Times* listed it as fifth coolest."

"I didn't know they ranked restaurants on the basis of cool."

"They do. It's part of the ambience rating."

"Is the food as good as the ambience?"

"I think so."

I lifted my menu. "What should I order?"

"I'd recommend the scallops or the lobster

204

linguini, but I haven't had anything I didn't like."

A few moments later the waitress returned with our appetizers and drinks. I dove into the calamari. It was lightly fried and fresh.

"This is divine," I said.

"After I terrified you with stories of human-eating squid, I thought you might find it empowering to eat some."

I popped a ring into my mouth. "You're right. I do feel powerful."

He ate some himself, then said, "It couldn't get much fresher. They probably pulled it up just miles from here. I love calamari, but usually by the time it reaches Utah, it's turned to rubber. You might as well be eating elastic bands."

"I know," I said. "But this is amazing. And I love that they serve it with pecorino. It's one of my favorite cheeses."

"I keep forgetting that you're a professional foodie."

"I think I've tried it all."

"Which will only make you harder to please."

"I'm not hard to please," I said. "I'm just . . . discriminating."

"Hopefully we're still just talking about food."

I took a drink, then looked at him and smiled. "Maybe."

Our waitress returned a few minutes later to take our orders.

"Do you know what you'd like?" Andrew asked.

"I'll have the scallops," I said. "With the house salad."

"And I will have the lobster linguini," Andrew said.

We handed the woman our menus and she walked away.

"This restaurant was started thirty years ago by an Italian man. His name was Giorgio, so he named it Ristorante da Giorgio. Not especially original, but it was very popular until a hurricane hit in 1991 and wiped it out.

"The next year he sold what was left of it to a group of Italian businessmen, who rebuilt and renamed it. It's been the hot thing ever since." He looked at me. "So many schemes, so many people looking for the next thing." He took a drink of his champagne. "That's what makes the world go round."

"Speaking of schemes," I said, smiling, "have you decided what you're going to do after the Christmas season?"

"I have a few ideas. Like I said, I've always got a plan."

"In Utah?"

He was quiet a moment, then said, "I don't know. Some of that depends on my brother. We may go back into business together."

"Then you might move?"

"It's a possibility."

I must have looked sad because he said, "You could always come with me."

"I'll have to think on that."

"*Think* or *drink*?"

I laughed. "Both."

He was quiet for a moment, then said, "If you don't want to follow me, I could always just have two families."

My jaw dropped. "I can't believe you just said that."

"What? Too soon?" He started laughing. I hit him with my napkin, then started laughing myself. It was healing to laugh about it for a change.

An hour later, as the sun began to sink into the Pacific, a loud gong sounded, followed by the bass tone of blowing conch shells. Before I could ask what was going on, Andrew said, "It's something they do every night. They say good night to the sun. It's their gimmick. That's where the restaurant got its name."

"That's cool," I said.

"Fifth coolest in the world," he replied.

After our meal we shared their specialty dessert, a *tartufo nero*—a decadent black truffle.

"Culinarily—" I started to say.

"Wait, is that a word?" Andrew asked.

"I just make up words sometimes," I said. "Culinarily, this may be the most unique Thanksgiving I've ever experienced. Except for the time my father cooked a raccoon for Thanksgiving dinner."

"You ate a raccoon?"

"My father lives by his own rule book."

"Clearly," Andrew said. His brow furrowed. "What does raccoon taste like?"

"Chicken, of course."

He laughed.

A minute later I said, "May I ask you something a little delicate?"

"I might not answer, but you can ask."

"Why do you love me?"

My question clearly surprised him. "So you're onto me."

"Well, if you were trying to hide it, you're not doing a very good job."

He breathed out slowly. "Well, I could tell you that I think you're the most beautiful woman in the world, but that would be shallow, wouldn't it? And it wouldn't be completely true either."

"Then I'm not the most beautiful woman in the world?" I asked lightly.

"No, you are," he said, smiling, "but that's not the *complete* reason I've fallen for you." He paused and I sensed he was taking my question seriously. "When I was a young man, I was motivated by approbation. The prize. That's the message culture showers on us, men and women. It's in every television show, movie, magazine. Men marry for looks, women marry for situations, both equally exploitative."

"Like that couple on the boat the other day," I said.

He nodded. "Tragically, that's what motivated my first marriage. Jamie was beautiful on the outside. Stunning. The kind of beautiful that made men stop what they were doing and gawk at her, then glare at me in envy.

"I liked it, maybe even thrived on it. It was proof that I was winning. But the trophy was plastic. Beautiful on the outside but empty on the inside makes for a hollow life. It took me a few years and a lot of scars to get there, but I learned that what I really wanted was someone who was real. Someone with her own battle scars from fighting life. I had to lose a lot to get there, but I'm grateful for it. It's like the scales have fallen off my eyes. Now, there are a lot of beautiful women who look ugly to me."

"So that blonde on the boat didn't interest you at all," I teased.

He grinned. "I'm not a eunuch," he said. "There was a time when I would have eaten up her attention. But my marriage changed that. What I mostly saw was how she disrespected the man she was with. I suppose they were disrespecting each other. But I just don't have any interest in that game anymore." He looked into my eyes. "The first time I met you, I saw this beautiful, strong woman with vulnerability in her eyes. Someone who was doing her best to muddle through the storm. I was attracted to that."

"You saw all that the first time you met me?"

He nodded. "A soldier friend of mine who had seen heavy combat told me that he could spot another combat veteran a mile away. He said that once you've been in battle, you're different. I suppose it's like that in love as well."

"You've been in battle?"

"Unfortunately."

"I'm sorry."

"I was too. But I'm not now. It's what it took to bring me to this place."

"And where is that?"

"With you."

It was nearly midnight when we returned to the condo. Andrew walked me to my room, then turned to go. "Don't leave," I said.

He looked at me. "You know . . ."

"You don't need to say it," I said. "Just lie with me until I fall asleep. I don't want you to leave me."

He thought for a moment. "Okay."

"Just give me a minute." I went into my bathroom, changed into a T-shirt and pajama shorts, then pulled down the covers and climbed onto the bed. Andrew took off his shirt and shoes, then lay down next to me. "Will you hold me?" I asked.

"Yes."

He lay back and I cuddled into him, my head against his bare chest, his strong arms wrapped around me. I felt so safe and happy and loved. "Never leave me," I said softly.

"Never," he said back.

The night faded into perfect fiction.

CHAPTER
Twenty-Nine

Love is just smoke and mirrors.
—Maggie Walther's Diary

I woke the next morning next to him. He was still asleep, his warm breath washing over me. I lay there, feeling him.

Before coming to Mexico I had wondered what awful thing I might discover about Andrew on this trip—which was more revealing of me than of him. What I'd discovered was that he was who he was. I still knew little of his past, but I knew his present. He was kind and vulnerable, honest and loving, not just to me but to others. No wonder the Mexican people loved him. No wonder I loved him.

I kissed his neck and he stirred a little. I looked up into his face and kissed him on the chin, then nestled back into him. I never wanted to leave this place—physically or emotionally.

"What time is it?" he asked softly.

"It's almost eight. What time do we have to leave?"

"Ten."

"I wish we didn't have to go."

"I think that every time I'm here," he said softly. "Not so much this time."

"How come?"

"This time, the best part is coming back with me."

I pressed my lips against his. Then I put my head on his chest and he pulled me in tight. "We have an hour," he said.

"An hour," I echoed.

I didn't fall back asleep. I didn't want to miss any of the moment. As I lay there I began thinking of the past year and this sudden juncture. Where would we go from here? I knew where I wanted to go. I wanted to join my life with his and fight life's battles together. That's what he said he was looking for. Is that really what he wanted?

I silenced my mind. There would be time to think about that later, and the clock was moving too fast as it was. It seemed like only minutes before he stirred, looking over at the clock next to the bed.

"Is it time?" I asked.

He kissed my forehead. "Yes."

I sighed heavily. "All good things must come to an end."

He rubbed his hand along my cheek. "Not all things." He kissed me and slowly sat up. "I'm going to shower." He got up, picked up his shirt and shoes, and walked out of my room.

I showered as well, then packed my things. I

pulled my coat from the closet, a symbol of what I'd left behind and what I was returning to. Yet it didn't seem so awful now. There was suddenly a warmth and strength inside me that felt greater than anything winter could throw at me.

My alarm clock said five minutes to ten. Time to go. I walked out into the living room. "I'm ready," I said.

Andrew was waiting for me on the sofa. "You're sure you didn't forget anything?"

"Pretty sure," I said. "If I did we'll just have to come back."

He smiled. Suddenly his expression changed. "I almost forgot our passports," he said, shaking his head. "That would have been bad. And I forgot to leave Jazmín a tip. Our passports are in that top drawer on the far right there," he said, pointing. "Next to the pantry. I put them under the papers so no one would find them. Would you grab them?"

"No problem," I said.

"I always leave Jazmín's tip in my top drawer, just to be safe." As he left the room, I went to the counter and opened the drawer. There was pile of official-looking papers inside. I rooted through them until I found our passports. As I brought them out, I noticed the top paper in the drawer. It had a graphic of an electric bolt and a green bar running across the top that read AVISO RECEIBO.

CFE Comisión Federal de Electricidad
Sr. Andrew Hill

The electric bill. I thought nothing of it as I shut the drawer. Then it struck me. It was addressed to Andrew Hill. Why was the electric bill in Andrew's name? And if it was Andrew's condo, why would he lie about it?

An anxious chill ran up my spine. Was I being lied to again? I pushed the thought aside. *There's an explanation,* I told myself. Maybe he was just being modest.

After all the lies and deceit I'd been through with Clive, was I a fool not to worry? Why would he lie to me? Anxiety flooded in like groundwater.

Andrew walked back into the room, replacing his wallet to his back pocket. "Did you find them?"

I shut the drawer, feeling guilty, as if I'd been caught doing something I shouldn't have been doing. I held the passports up. "Right here."

"Good." He looked around, then breathed out. "Well, off we go. Back to the snow."

"I haven't even checked the weather," I said, trying to talk about something else besides what was on my mind.

"I did," he said. "It snowed twice while we were gone. At this rate, Salt Lake will be a glacier by the end of winter."

"We should stay here," I said. I think I meant it more than either of us suspected. Something told me that when this weekend was gone, it was really gone.

Andrew kissed me on the forehead. "We'll come back soon."

I closed my eyes as he kissed me. I know it was stupid—most fear usually is—but I just couldn't get the electric bill off my mind. *Why would he lie?*

CHAPTER
Thirty

Before taking this trip, I was afraid that I would come home with a man I no longer cared about. Instead, I came home *without* a man whom I care too much about.
—Maggie Walther's Diary

It was a longer ride to the airport than I remembered. Andrew and I hardly spoke, though he didn't seem bothered by my silence. He probably just thought I was quiet because we were going back home. I wished that were the case. It was true, of course, but the greater reason for my silence was the fear that had commandeered my thoughts. Several times I glanced over at Andrew and he suddenly looked like a stranger to me. I loved him. Why wasn't that enough? But I had loved Clive too. And trusted him. And where had that gotten me?

The trip had raised more questions than it answered. Andrew wasn't who I thought he was when we first met—a simple man in boots and worn Levis, working at a Christmas tree lot to keep the lights on. He had money, sophistication, intelligence, and a past whose surface I'd only begun to scratch. Who was he?

What seemed innocent before now scared me. Clive was about Clive. Our marriage was *The Clive Show*, and he had the spotlight and star billing while the rest of us were relegated to supporting roles or the studio audience. Personality-wise, Andrew was the polar opposite of Clive. He genuinely seemed more interested in me than in himself. At first I found this endearing. Now I was afraid that he was hiding something.

Or am I just being paranoid? If anyone had reason to be paranoid, it was me. I didn't even trust myself anymore. My husband had been able to keep another wife and family from me for three years. Clearly I was far more gullible than I ever dared believe.

My emotions blurred like the desert landscape around us, turning from fear to anger then to self-hate for undermining what seemed to be my greatest chance at happiness. This had been the perfect week. Andrew had been nothing but fun, generous, and loving. Why wasn't that enough?

We returned our car to the airport rental lot and took a shuttle to the terminal. The airport was insanely crowded with foreigners returning home from the holiday.

When it was our turn to check in, I followed Andrew up to the ticket counter, where he handed the gate agent—a mustached, ruddy-faced Mexican man—both of our passports. The badge on the man's chest read Javier de la Cruz.

The man opened the first passport, then glanced up at me. "Mrs. Walther?" he said in clear English.

I stepped forward. "I'm Mrs. Walther."

"Okay. Do you have luggage?"

"Yes," I said.

"Please put it here," he said, pointing to the opening next to his counter.

Andrew lifted my bag onto the scale while the agent printed out my boarding pass. He put a label on my bag and set it on the conveyer belt behind him.

Then Andrew set his own bag on the scale. "This is mine," he said.

The agent printed out another boarding pass, then slapped a label on Andrew's bag and also set it on the belt behind him.

"Here is your boarding pass, *Señora*," he said to me, handing me my ticket with my passport. "You will be departing from gate twelve." Then he turned to Andrew and did the same. "Here is your passport, *Señor*. You will be at gate seventeen."

I looked at Andrew. "Why are we at different gates?"

Andrew turned to me. "I'm sorry. I forgot to tell you, I'm flying straight to Denver. It was the only way I could stay here this long. I need to be in Denver tomorrow morning."

"To visit family," I said.

He looked at me peculiarly. "I told you I go to Denver every Saturday."

I don't know what it was, but this only added to my fear. My eyes began to well up. I turned and started walking toward security. Andrew came after me. "Maggie?" He grabbed my arm, then walked in front of me. "What's wrong?"

I looked at him, fighting to keep my composure. "Why didn't you tell me?"

"I'm sorry. I just forgot. It was an honest mistake." *Honest.* I suddenly hated that word. Andrew just looked at me with a concerned expression. "I don't understand. Why are you so upset?"

"I don't do well with secrets," I said.

Andrew's brow furrowed. "This wasn't a secret, Maggie. I just forgot to tell you. Do you think I'm hiding something?"

I took a deep breath, fighting back emotion. Then I looked at him. "I'm sorry. I'm just emotional. It's hard going home."

"I understand," he said. He took my hand. "We better get through security before we miss our flights."

We went through the security line, which even in priority took nearly thirty minutes. I tried to act calm, even though anxiety was building inside me like a pressure cooker. Why couldn't I shut it off?

When we got to my gate, Andrew said, "It

looks like they've already started boarding." He breathed out slowly. "Look, I'm really sorry I didn't tell you, Maggie. I should have been more thoughtful." He took out his wallet. "You're going to need a ride home from the airport." He offered me a hundred-dollar bill. "That's for an Uber."

"I don't need money," I said. "I'll get a ride."

"Maggie, please."

I looked at him, unable to hold back the question that was haunting me. "Whose condo did we just stay in?"

He looked at me blankly. "Why are you asking me that?"

"The electric bill was in your name."

I could see that my question threw him. "Is that really why you're upset?"

"I don't do secrets," I said again.

He looked at me for a moment, then said, "Neither do I." He took a deep breath. "You better get on your flight." Even though he was upset, he kissed me on the cheek. "Remember I love you."

"I know," I said softly.

"I hope you do."

I didn't reply. He breathed out slowly. "Call me when you get home so I know you're safe." Then he turned and walked away. I watched him disappear into a river of humanity as a tear rolled down my cheek. He was the best thing that had happened to me in years. Maybe ever. And I had no idea who he really was.

I was a mess on the flight home. I kept bursting into tears. After my second breakdown, the elderly Mexican man sitting next to me asked if I were okay. I told him I was, then started crying again. He got a box of Kleenex from the flight attendant for me.

I thought of texting Carina for a ride home but I didn't want to explain my emotional state. I wasn't even sure that I could. After all he'd done, I felt so ungrateful. Still, as perfect as everything had been in Cabo, a part of me now wished that I hadn't gone. I just wanted to retreat to my house, lock my doors, and hibernate for the rest of the winter.

My Uber delivered me to my neighborhood around four in the afternoon. The city looked like Antarctica. We drove down a long white corridor, as the snowplows had left the road lined on both sides with snowdrifts nearly five feet high. Once inside, I left my bag in the kitchen and went straight to bed.

CHAPTER
Thirty-One

Am I protecting or sabotaging myself? I honestly don't know anymore. I feel like I don't know anything anymore—especially how much more of this I can take.
—Maggie Walther's Diary

I slept for a couple of hours, then woke and tossed and turned until around midnight, when I finally got up and took two Ambien with a glass of wine. I didn't wake until noon the next day.

I woke with a pounding headache. I looked at my clock, then got out of bed. I walked over to the window and opened the blinds. It was gray outside, the sun burning pale orange behind a thick curtain of clouds.

I felt like I was suffering from an emotional hangover. In the light of a new day I felt like a crazy woman—like the Clive-induced PTSD of the last year had left small land mines on my heart just waiting for someone to trigger them. Unfortunately, that someone had been Andrew. Why had I gotten so angry that he had to fly to Denver? Why would I accuse him of hiding something, when he had already told me that he went to Denver every week? And why was something as simple as an electric bill freaking me out? There could be a dozen plausible explanations. At least. Why couldn't I have just given him a little grace?

In the previous day's emotional state, I had forgotten to call Andrew to tell him I'd arrived home. My phone had been off since our flight to Cabo. I turned it back on, hoping that there was a message from Andrew. After all my drama, I doubted there would be, but I hoped.

Just seconds after turning my phone back on, it began beeping with voicemails and text messages. Carina alone had left three of the former and six of the latter. There were two voicemail messages from Clive as well. Then I saw the text message Andrew had sent late last night. I went directly to it.

ANDREW
I hope you got home safe.

Thank you again for such a beautiful time.

I hope you will forgive me for not telling you about my Denver flight. I'm back around six.

Would you like to get together?

I breathed out in relief. Then I typed back.

MAGGIE
I'm sorry I was so upset. Yes, I can't wait to see you. I hope YOU will forgive me. Love, me

I felt both relief and shame. Relief that he hadn't given up on me and shame that I had given him reason to. I scrolled back on my phone to read my other texts. They had started coming on Thursday.

CARINA
Happy Thanksgiving, doll. Hope you're having a good time down south. P.S. I had to buy a dozen new tablecloths.
I'll explain later.

CARINA
Hi there. Call me when you can.

CLIVE
You there? I left you a voicemail.

CLIVE
Mag?

CARINA
Hey, doll. Are you back?

CARINA
Worried, please call.

CARINA

I thought you were coming back today.
Please call. We need to talk. Important.

CARINA

Should I file a missing persons report?

I ignored Clive's pleas but listened to the last of Carina's voicemails. She sounded upset. "Honey, please call me as soon as you can. I have something important to tell you."

I immediately dialed her number. Carina answered on the first ring. "Finally," she said, making no attempt to conceal her exasperation. "Where in the world are you?"

"I'm home. I got back yesterday."

"Why didn't you call me? I've been worried out of my head. I probably left you a dozen messages."

"Nine," I said. "Sorry. I forgot that I turned my phone off. What's going on?"

"I need to talk to you."

"Yes?"

"In person. We need to talk in person."

"Why? Is it bad?"

She didn't answer, which I guess was an answer.

"So it's serious," I said.

"I think so."

I sighed. I really didn't need or want any more drama in my life. "All right," I said. "Where do you want to meet?"

"Coffee in twenty," she said.

"Give me forty. I just got up."

"Forty," she said. "Bye."

It took me a half hour to get ready. I felt heartsick knowing she had bad news. My mind ran the gamut of possible disasters, from finding out that a client was suing us to Carina quitting.

When I got to the coffee shop, Carina was sitting in a corner as far from humanity as possible. For once she looked unmade, her hair pulled back into a ponytail; her eyes, sans mascara, were rimmed with dark circles. Her appearance only added to my anxiety. She stood as I approached and hugged me. "I'm so glad you're back. I got you a grande. I hope that's okay."

"Thank you," I said, sitting down. "So, my heart's pounding out of my chest. What's so important?"

"How was your trip?" she asked.

"It was perfect."

"And Andrew?"

"He was perfect."

She looked more surprised than pleased. "Did he tell you much about himself? About his past?"

"A little. He was married before. He worked in finance but had some business problems just before he moved here from Colorado."

"Did he tell you why he had to move?"

"He didn't have to move," I said. "He said he had some business problems." Carina just shook her head. Her coyness made me angry.

"What is it you're dying to tell me?" I said.

Carina took in a deep breath, then reached into her purse. She brought out a sheet of paper and set it in front of me. It was a copy of a newspaper article she had printed off the Internet. The photograph accompanying the article froze my heart. It was a picture of Andrew being led away in handcuffs.

Denver Man Found Guilty in $32 Million Investment Fraud

Denver investment fund manager Aaron Hill was found guilty on six counts of investment fraud after transferring nearly $32 million in investors' funds into offshore bank accounts. Hill cooperated with security agents, who were able to locate and return all but $75,000 of the investors' capital. Hill was the CEO and founder of Hill & Associates, an investment company.

A federal judge ordered Hill to repay the debt and sentenced him to three and a half years in prison with parole eligibility in 24 months. Hill's sentence will begin on December 6. He will be incarcerated in the Englewood Federal Correctional Institution, a low-security facility for nonviolent offenders.

I looked up at Carina, my heart pounding wildly. "This man's name is Aaron."

"But's that him, right?"

I looked again at the picture. It was definitely Andrew. The article was dated December 3, 2014, almost two years earlier.

"He must have changed his name," Carina said.

"Where did you find this?"

"On the Internet. I googled him and this came up." She looked at me anxiously. "There's more."

She set down another paper.

Wife of Convicted Fund Manager Alleges Assault

Convicted fund manager Aaron Hill is being sued by his former wife for $2 million for assault and battery. Hill has recently been convicted of six counts of fraud after embezzling nearly $32 million from his firm's clients. Hill declined to comment, but his attorney said that his client denies the accusations and deserves his day in a court of law, rather than trial by misinformed public opinion.

I started to cry. Carina reached in her purse and brought out a tissue. "I'm so sorry, honey. I hate that I had to be the one to tell you. At least now you know why he's gone every weekend."

"What do you mean?"

"He probably has to go back to Colorado each week to check in with his parole officer."

I rested my head in my palm. Tears streamed down my cheek and fell to the table. Carina slid her chair over next to me. "I'm so sorry, honey."

"Every time I think I've found something I can trust, it's false. I thought Clive was the ideal husband. Now Andrew . . ."

"Aaron," Carina said.

"Whatever his name is," I snapped.

"It's okay, honey. You have every right to be angry."

"What am I doing to attract this?"

"It's not you." She rubbed my back. "It's not your fault. When do you see him next?"

"Tonight."

Carina's brow furrowed. "What are you going to do?"

"I don't know." I lifted the articles. "Can I take these?"

"Of course."

For a moment we were both silent. Then I said, "I've got to go."

"Call me tonight after you see him," Carina

said. "Or whenever. Any time day or night. I'm here for you."

We hugged, then I followed her out of the cafe, holding back a torrent of emotions until I was in my own car. Then I leaned against the steering wheel and sobbed.

CHAPTER
Thirty-Two

I sent him away.

> —Maggie Walther's Diary

I cried most of the afternoon. I didn't know what I should do. Should I confront him about what Carina had told me? Did I even have the strength to?

Andrew arrived a little after seven. He looked tired from travel but happy to see me. I'm pretty sure that I looked like emotional roadkill. I only partially opened the door.

"Hi," he said, his expression changing at seeing me.

I sniffed. "Hi."

"Are you all right?"

I shook my head.

"What's wrong?"

I swallowed. "I just don't feel well. It's been an awful day."

"Did something else happen?"

I didn't answer.

"Did I do something?" I still didn't answer. He looked at me for a moment, then said, "Do you want me to leave?"

I was seriously conflicted. I wanted him to

comfort and protect me from him. Finally I said, "That would probably be best."

"All right." He looked at me. "Are you sure that's all that's wrong?"

I hesitated for a second, then said, "Yes."

He looked at me doubtfully. "All right. I'll call you tomorrow. Good night."

He had started to step back when I said, "Where do you go every weekend?"

He looked at me for a moment. "You know where I go. Denver."

"Why?"

"To see my brother."

"Why?"

His eyes reflected his hurt. "Because it's the only time I can." Neither of us spoke for a moment, then he said, "I don't know what I've done to make you distrust me, but something's happened." His voice cracked a little. "Don't think this is easy for me either. Maggie, you're not the only one who has reason not to trust."

For a moment his words just hung in the air between us, then he looked as if he were going to say something but stopped himself. He just turned and walked away. Something in my heart told me to go after him, but I didn't. I went back to my room and cried.

The next three days passed in a lifeless funk. While the world around me glistened with holiday tinsel, my heart was as dark inside as I kept my house. I didn't even plug in my Christmas tree lights. The title of a book I'd read decades ago came to mind: *The Winter of Our Discontent*. That's what this felt like—the winter of my discontent. And it seemed like this winter would never end.

Andrew didn't call. Clive did. Three times. I didn't answer. I just wanted him to go away. Part of me blamed him for what had happened between Andrew and me. Had he not broken my trust, I wouldn't have been so untrusting. Or had he done me a favor? Like I said, I was conflicted. Then, late Monday, he texted me something cryptic.

CLIVE
It is what it is.
Don't worry about coming to trial.

I almost called him back to see what he meant. I didn't have to. I found out soon enough.

CHAPTER
Thirty-Three

Someone threw a brick through my window. I'm afraid. What is wrong with people? Why can't they just live their own lives?

—Maggie Walther's Diary

My cell phone rang around six a.m. I rolled over and checked the caller ID before answering.

"Carina?"

"Are you up?" she asked.

"I am now."

"Have you seen today's paper?"

"I just woke."

"Clive had another family."

It took a moment for her words to gel. "What?"

"He had a third wife and three other children."

I was stunned. "Where?"

"Spanish Fork, Utah."

My already battered heart felt like it had just been delivered another sucker punch. More betrayal. More evidence of my stupidity. And still to come, more media circus. It was going to start all over again. Why wouldn't it end? I knew the answer. It wouldn't end until Clive stopped giving the media juicy things to report on. Or until it stopped selling newspapers.

"What are you going to do?" Carina asked.

"What is there to do?" I said. "Board up the windows for another storm."

Ironically, my words were answered by the crash of a breaking window.

"What was that?" Carina asked.

I pulled on my robe and ran into the front room. There was a large hole in my picture window, and my carpet was covered with shards of glass. In the center of my living room floor was a brick. It took me a moment to understand what I was seeing.

"Maggie? Are you okay?"

"Someone just threw a brick through my window. I need to call the police."

"Do you want me to come over?"

"I've got to go." I hung up and dialed 911. Then I sat down in my kitchen to wait for the police. How much worse was this going to get?

Ten minutes later my doorbell rang. It was a police officer. He looked boyish but was thickly built. I thought he appeared too young for the uniform.

"You called in a broken window?" he said.

"Yes."

"May I come in?"

"Yes."

I pulled open the door. He stepped inside and

looked at the glass covering my carpeted floor. "I'm Officer Huber," he said. He walked over and examined the brick. "Is this what they threw through the window?"

No, I always keep a brick in the middle of my living room floor. "It would appear so," I said.

"Have you touched it?"

"No. That's where it was."

He took out a pad and wrote something down. "When did you notice the window was broken?"

"When I heard it," I said. "About fifteen minutes ago."

"So you were here when it happened?"

"I was in my bedroom."

"Did you hear a car or motorcycle drive away?"

"No. I only heard the window break."

"Is there any other damage to your property?"

"I don't know. I haven't been out. Not that I'm aware of."

"Do you have any surveillance cameras around the house?"

"No."

"How about your neighbors?"

"I wouldn't know."

He nodded. "I'll check with them, see if they saw anything." He again wrote something down. "Is there anyone you know of who is upset with you?"

"Not that I know of."

"A boyfriend or ex-husband. This kind of vandalism is usually perpetrated by someone the victim knows."

"They're both upset with me," I said, more to myself than the officer. He looked at me with interest. "But they wouldn't do this."

He lifted his pad. "I'd better take their names."

"My husband was in the newspaper this morning. I think this may have something to do with him."

"Then you think he did it."

"No, I think someone who doesn't like him did it. He's a former city councilman. Clive Walther. He was arrested for bigamy."

"Councilman Walther," he said. "I know about his arrest." He again wrote something on his pad. "And this boyfriend?"

"He's not really a boyfriend. I don't want you contacting him. It would be embarrassing."

"You never know."

"He wouldn't do this. I don't want you contacting him."

A few minutes later there was another knock on the door. "That should be the detective," Officer Huber said. "May I let him in?"

"Yes."

He opened the door. A thin, bald man wearing an oversized down vest stepped inside my house. He held a camera in one hand and had a black, box-shaped bag hanging at his side.

"This is Mrs. Walther," Officer Huber said.

"I'm Detective Frederickson," he said to me. "I'm sorry this happened. I'm just going to take a few pictures for our records, then dust for fingerprints."

"Fine," I said, stepping back.

The detective walked over to the brick. "This is what was thrown through the window?"

"Yes."

"Have you touched it?"

"She hasn't," Officer Huber said.

"No," I said. "Can you take fingerprints off a brick?"

"Sometimes. Or DNA." He leaned over and took a picture of the brick, then stooped down and brushed it with powder.

I sat down on the couch and watched the police work as if I were watching a crime show on TV. My living room was as cold as my refrigerator and getting colder. I could see my breath.

"I'm going to talk to your neighbors," Officer Huber said. He pointed to the broken window. "You might want to hang something over that."

After he left, I asked the detective if I could hang something over the window.

"Just a minute," he replied. He took a few pictures of the window, then said, "Okay, I'm good."

I got some duct tape from the garage and a quilt from the hall closet and brought them into the living room. I tried to hang the quilt myself but failed.

"Excuse me; could you give me a hand?" I asked the detective.

He glanced up at me from the floor. "Sure thing."

He left his kit on the floor and came to the window. I got up on a chair and he held the quilt in place as I taped it around the sides of the window, darkening the room. I could still feel the cold coming through, but at least it was better than it was. I turned on the room light and started a fire in the fireplace.

The detective walked around my living room taking pictures for another few minutes, then said, "All right. I'm done here. Thank you."

"Thank you," I replied. I let him out the door.

Fifteen minutes later Officer Huber returned. I was in the kitchen making myself some toast when he knocked, then slightly opened the door. "Mrs. Walther?"

I walked back to the living room. "You can come in."

He stepped inside. "I visited with your neighbors. None of them saw anything or have functional surveillance cameras." He took a business card from his shirt pocket and wrote on it. "Here's my info and your case number for your insurance. You'll need it to file a homeowner's claim. What's the best number to reach you at?"

"My cell." I gave him my number.

"If I find anything, we'll give you a call."

"Do you think you will?"

He frowned. "We'll do our best. Have a good day."

He walked out. I went back to the kitchen to get my toast, which was now too cold to melt butter. I had just put it back in the toaster when there was another knock on my door.

"What did they forget now?" I said to myself. I walked back out and opened it. A young woman with a pixie cut stood on the doorstep.

"Hi, Mrs. Walther? I'm from the *Herald*. We received a report that someone threw a brick through your window. Is your husband Councilman Walther here?"

"No. And that's ex-councilman and ex-husband. He was removed from the council, and we're divorced."

She lifted her pad. "So you believe that this act of violence was directed at you?"

"Why would someone throw a brick through my window because my husband cheated on me?"

"I really don't know," she said.

"Neither do I. Good-bye." I shut the door with her still standing there. I went back to the kitchen. My toast was charred and smoking. I threw it away and started over. I was finally eating toast when the doorbell rang again.

I groaned. "Just leave me alone." I walked out and opened the door. An elderly man stood at my doorstep. It took me a moment to recognize him as my neighbor, Mr. Stephens. He had a roll of plastic tucked under one arm and a roll of duct tape in his hand.

"Mrs. Walther, I'm Bryan Stephens from across the street."

"Mr. Stephens," I said. "Please come in."

"Call me Bryan," he said as he stepped inside. "A police officer just came by to ask if we'd seen who threw a brick through your window."

"I'm sorry he disturbed you so early in the morning."

"It's no problem," he said. "I've always been an early riser. I was just having coffee and doing a crossword puzzle. Only thing the newspaper's any good for these days. I'm sorry we couldn't be of assistance to the officer. But I figured you probably could use someone to patch your window." He looked over at the window. "I see you put a blanket up."

"It's all I had," I said. "It's not working too well."

"I've got this plastic painting tarp. It will seal up nicely until you can get someone to replace the glass. And it will still let some light into the room."

"Thank you," I said. "You're too kind."

"I'm just glad to still be of use."

"Do you need some help?"

"Nah, this is easy stuff."

He took off his shoes and laid the plastic roll on the floor. He pulled down my quilt and measured the window with a tape measure. Then he rolled out a long, rectangular piece of plastic and cut it with a razor knife.

Watching him work reminded me of my father. He was good with his hands and was always repairing things—something Clive never did. The truth was, Clive was domestically challenged. When we first got married, he'd call a plumber if the toilet got clogged. I had to show him how to use a plunger.

"May I get you some coffee?" I asked.

"That would be nice. Just black, please. Or maybe a couple spoonfuls of milk if you have it."

A few minutes later, when I brought out his coffee, my quilt was neatly folded on the couch and he had already taped the sides of the plastic to the window.

"This plastic is good material. I got it twelve years ago when I was remodeling the basement. It's hard to find plastic this thick anymore. It's nearly twenty mils."

I had no idea what that meant but I nodded appreciatively. Then he precariously climbed up on a chair to seal the top of the window.

"You sure I can't do that?" I said.

"I've got it."

When he finished sealing the plastic, there was no more cold air coming through. I set down his coffee, then took his hand and helped him down from the chair.

"I'll take that coffee now."

"You've earned it," I said, handing him the cup. He sat down on the couch and sipped it. "This is good coffee."

"Thank you. It's a local roaster."

"I put your blanket right here." He patted the quilt.

"Thank you," I said. "You even folded it."

He took a few more sips, then looked at the window. "Yes, that's some quality Visqueen there. Like I said, it's good thick stuff. It's got an R-factor close to window glass, maybe even a four."

Again, I had no idea what he was talking about.

"Thank you," I said. "You're very kind."

"That's what neighbors are for," he replied. He took another sip of coffee. "Yes, that's a fine brew. You'll have to tell Leisa what kind it is when she brings your plates back. Those cookies you baked for us sure were tasty."

"I'm glad you liked them," I said. "I was so sorry to learn about your son."

His expression fell. He set down his coffee and said, "That tape should hold a few weeks, but I wouldn't put off replacing the window too long." He stood. "I best get back to Leisa. She gets worried if I stay too long at a pretty girl's house. And she's got her own honey-do list I need to get started on." He put his hand through the roll of duct tape, lifted the roll of plastic, and walked to the door. "Have a good day," he said. "And have a happy holiday."

"To you too," I said. "And your wife."

"I'll pass on your sentiments."

I watched him carefully make his way down my icy walk. Then I shut the door behind him. *What a kind, broken man,* I thought.

CHAPTER
Thirty-Four

Once again, my life needs a reset button.
—Maggie Walther's Diary

I spent the rest of the day in bed reading, doing my best to escape the new reality I'd been tossed headlong into. I didn't know if I could go through this all over again. I didn't want to isolate myself anymore; I just wanted to run as far away as possible. I started thinking about moving out of state. Maybe I should have thought of it before; I just didn't know where I'd go. At first, all I could think of was Cabo, which only made me feel worse.

I considered going back to Ashland. I knew Ashland might be hell, but it was, at least, a hell I was familiar with. And, right now, it couldn't be as bad as Salt Lake. At least strangers in Ashland wouldn't pass any judgment on my life.

I hadn't seen my father for nine years—not since my wedding. I wondered what he was like now. I've seen men mellow as they age. I'm sure a psychiatrist would have had a field day with this, but I suppose some part of me still wanted to earn his approval. Or maybe the idea of going back was just another form of self-flagellation for all my poor decisions.

I wondered what my father would say if I came back. Most likely it would be some type of "I told you so." He wouldn't even have to say it: it would just shine from his eyes. He loved being proved right. He used to say, "I'm never wrong. It's the facts that get mixed up."

He had never liked Clive, though that didn't surprise me. Clive wasn't his type of man. In fact, he didn't consider him a man. My father called him "a slick-boy politician with a pretty mouth," which I'm sure was one of the worst insults Dad could think of. The morning of my wedding he said to me, "That pretty boy of yours needs to spend a week on the side of a mountain with me hunting bear. That'll grow him some chest hair."

My father was big on chest hair. When I was younger—before I physically matured—he was always saying things would "grow me chest hair." When I told him I didn't want chest hair, he just laughed. "Why not, you ain't got nothing else on it."

Was I really considering going back to that? Was I that desperate? It was like most of my life: my plans weren't about where I was going but about what I was running from. The cycle just continued. I was ready to give it all up— my home, my business, my life in Utah—just to escape the daily reminders of pain, reminders which had started with Clive but had since moved on to another man.

Andrew. Or Aaron, or whatever his name was. I couldn't stop thinking about him. It's easy to say that the pain of losing him was disproportionate to the time I had known him, but hearts don't always work like that. I have seen people walk away from fifty-year-old marriages without looking back, and I've seen hearts broken over week-long affairs. I had only known him for three weeks and my heart felt truly in peril. I had fallen in deep. Still, it was better to lose him now than later. I once heard it said that "It's best to dismiss bad love at the door, instead of after it has moved into the heart and unpacked all its suitcases." Why couldn't he just have been who I thought he was?

Around midnight, I made plans to return to Oregon. I had no idea how long I would stay. Maybe a day, maybe forever. The drive was a little over seven hundred miles, which I could do in twelve hours. If I left at eight a.m., I would get there a few hours after dark. I decided I would leave on Sunday morning.

CHAPTER
Thirty-Five

I've made a big mistake. Again. I'm getting good at it.

—Maggie Walther's Diary

I called Carina the next morning to tell her I was leaving.

"How long will you be gone?" she asked.

"I don't know yet."

"You're not talking about a permanent move . . ."

"I don't know yet."

"I don't want to talk about this. You can't leave."

"There's no reason for me to stay."

"No reason? Your home is here."

"It doesn't feel like home anymore."

"You have your business."

"You're already handling that."

She sounded exasperated. "What about your friends?"

"There's just you," I said.

"Just?" she repeated. "That was hurtful."

"You know I didn't mean it like that."

There was a long pause, then Carina's voice

came in pained realization. "When are you leaving?"

"Sunday morning," I said.

"You're not even going to say good-bye?"

"I'll see you before I go. And I'll be back," I said. "There are things I'd need to do before I left for good. Business things. We'll have time together."

We were both silent for a moment, then Carina said, "I don't know what else to say. I understand why you want to leave. I couldn't go through what you're going through. I just think it's so wrong that you have to bear this."

"Life happens," I said. "By the way, I called Scott and told him to give you a Christmas bonus of all of November and December's profits."

"That's too much," Carina said.

"No. You earned it."

"Maggie?"

"Yes?"

"I hope you're not serious about staying in Oregon. You're not the only one short on friends."

We said good-bye and I went to shower. I was drying my hair when someone knocked on my door. (I don't know why almost no one used the doorbell. I'm not really complaining; it's just a mystery to me.) I quickly pulled on my jeans and sweater and walked out to the foyer, hoping it wasn't another reporter. I unbolted the door and opened it.

It was Andrew. He was wearing a leather jacket with a tweed scarf, his hands in his pockets. For a moment we just looked at each other.

"Hi," he said, his breath clouding before him.

"Hi," I returned softly.

He nervously cleared his throat. "I read about Clive in the paper. I just wanted to make sure you were all right."

I nodded. "I'm okay."

He sniffed. "Good. I just wanted to make sure."

"Do you want to come in?" I asked.

He looked at me cautiously. "You sure you want that?"

"No," I said. "Do you want to come in?"

He hesitated a moment, then stepped inside. Noticeably, he didn't hug or even touch me. I shut the door behind him. He looked over at my bandaged window. "The paper said someone threw a brick through your window."

I nodded. "Yeah. That was a nice addition to yesterday morning."

"You weren't hurt, were you?"

"No. Just frightened."

"I'm sorry. People are crazy."

"Would you like some coffee?" I asked.

"No, I was just dropping by on the way to work."

"I've missed you."

He looked like he didn't know how to respond.

After our last encounter I'm certain he was confused.

"I've missed you too."

"I'll make us some coffee."

We went into the kitchen. Andrew sat down at the table. "Did they catch who threw the brick?"

"No. I doubt they will."

"Whoever did it must have thought that Clive was still living here."

"I assume so. I don't know why anyone would want to throw a brick at me." I looked at him. "Except you. You probably want to throw a brick at me."

He didn't smile.

"That was a joke," I said.

He still didn't smile. I brought our coffee over and sat down. "The police asked me if I had an upset ex-husband or ex-boyfriend. I told him I had both. I wouldn't give him your name."

"Is that who I am? Your ex-boyfriend?"

I didn't know how to answer that. "I forgot your sugar." I got up, got the sugar tin, and carried it over to the table, then sat back down.

"Thank you," he said without looking at me. He took out two of my homemade sugar cubes and dropped them into his coffee. He drank for a moment in silence, then said, "What happened, Maggie? I don't know what's going on. I mean, you told me you loved me and now you won't talk to me."

"I know," I said softly. "It's complicated."

"I can do complicated. What I can't do is not knowing what I did wrong."

"You didn't do anything wrong," I said. I breathed out slowly. "I was afraid." I looked back up into his eyes. "I was afraid of getting hurt again. I've been hurt too much."

He gazed at me with a confused expression. "What made you think I would hurt you?"

"I don't know."

He leaned forward. "You can tell me."

I swallowed. "I'm afraid to tell you."

"What are you afraid of? Losing me? Because as things are, you already have."

Tears came to my eyes. Then I said, "Okay. I'll tell you."

He sat back in his chair.

I took a deep breath to compose myself. "It started the last day in Cabo when you sent me to get the passports. In that drawer, there was an electric bill with your name on it. I couldn't figure out why it was in your name. Then I wondered if it really was your condo and it made me think you were lying to me." I looked down. "It made me wonder what else you were hiding from me."

He thought for a moment. "And then I forgot to tell you about my flight to Denver." He took another swallow of coffee, then looked up at me and said, "The condo was part mine, once. Now it belongs to my brother."

"I should have just asked."

His expression didn't change. "There's more, isn't there?"

"Yes."

"Just tell me."

I felt like he was asking me to take a step off a very high cliff. I knew that once I was over the edge there was no turning back.

"Please," he said. "Give me a chance to explain."

I got up and walked to my room and retrieved the newspaper article that Carina had given me. I came back to the table and set it down in front of him.

He lifted the paper. He read through it, then set it back down. "I guess that explains it." He looked at me, his eyes dark and pained. "You think this is me?"

"It's your picture."

"Did you read the whole article?"

"Yes."

"Did you read the part that said his first chance at parole was in two years?" He pushed the article to me. "Look at the date of the article. It hasn't been two years yet. The man in the picture is still in prison." He sighed. "That's my brother. We're identical twins. He's being paroled in eight days. On the ninth."

For a moment I was speechless. "You're a twin?"

"Identical twins," he said.

How could I have been so stupid?

"Five years ago my brother and I started a business together. Hill Brothers Management. We were venture capitalists. We raised money for start-ups—risky, blue-sky opportunities. We were good at it, but Aaron was the brains behind it all. He had a sixth sense.

"Our first year in business we backed an investment that our investors weren't especially excited about—a little plastic gizmo that separates the wires on phone chargers. It did better than anyone expected. A lot better. Our client sold millions of them online at five dollars each. By the time everyone else started marketing their own version, he had sold more than twenty million units."

"I have one of those," I said.

"I know, I noticed it that night I brought your tree," he said. He settled a little in his chair. "We were riding pretty high. Everyone involved was making money. But some people can't leave well enough alone. Our investors got greedy, and since Aaron was making the most profit on these deals, they staged a coup and pushed him out of his own firm. Not both of us, just him."

"How could they do that?"

"It's complex," he said. "But the bottom line is, he was too trusting. It had never occurred to him that the people he had done the most for would be the first to turn on him."

His words made my stomach hurt. He could have been describing me.

"As if that wasn't bad enough, a week later he found out that his wife had been having an affair with one of the investors. Everyone he trusted had turned against him. Everyone.

"He was hurt, but he didn't quit. He started his own firm. Just him. With his record, investors threw money at him. But that's when things started to go wrong. Large amounts of money and a broken soul don't go well together. Things began to unravel. He started drinking heavily. Then, when his new projects weren't panning out, he started siphoning money to offshore accounts. He had moved over thirty million before he was caught."

"How was he caught?" I asked.

"He turned himself in. He didn't have the heart of a crook." He breathed out slowly. "His original company went under. That was no surprise. Aaron had always been the brains behind it. It had already started floundering soon after he left. Then, with all the media his trial generated, the Hill name wasn't just tarnished, it was poisoned. That's why I left the state. There was nothing I could do there."

I sat quietly processing it all. "How is your brother doing?"

"About as well as you would expect for someone in prison. Thankfully it's not the usual correctional facility filled with violent offenders, but it's still prison . . ." He suddenly got emotional. "I'm all the family he has. The only time I'm allowed to see him is visiting hours Saturday morning. That's why I go back to Denver every week."

I looked at him. "I didn't know."

"You just needed to ask," he said quietly.

"I was just so afraid that I was being lied to. I was so stupid."

Andrew sat quietly thinking, then he said, "No. You're not stupid. You were right to protect yourself. You deserve the truth." He abruptly stood. "You were right, Maggie. This never could have worked." He walked to the door.

I was stunned. I got up and went after him, stopping him as he opened the door. "Andrew, I'm sorry. I know I screwed up. Please give me another chance. Please. I love you."

"You don't really know me."

"I do know you. I've seen your heart."

He looked at me with sad, vacant eyes, then took a deep breath. "What if I had been the one who stole the money? Knowing who I am now, would you have given me another chance? Could you have forgiven me?"

I thought for a moment, then said, "I don't know. But it wasn't you. It's not important."

His frown deepened. "It's more important than you think." He kissed me on the cheek, then turned and walked out the door. Now I was the one in the dark. Something told me I would never see him again.

CHAPTER
Thirty-Six

I wish I wasn't so good at getting in the way of my own happiness.
—Maggie Walther's Diary

Late afternoon the following day, Carina sat quietly at the kitchen table across from me. She had come directly to my home from catering a wedding rehearsal lunch and was still wearing her black serving tunic. The newspaper article lay on the table between us.

"So he's an identical twin," she finally said. "Do you believe him?"

Her question angered me. "Aaron Hill, his twin brother, is still in prison," I said. "It's public record. It's right there in the article. With all our genius, we somehow missed that little detail."

"All my genius," Carina said. "It's my fault."

"That's why Andrew goes back to Colorado every Saturday: to see his brother. He drives almost ten hours each way just to visit with his brother for a few minutes. I should have sainted him, not demonized him."

"You couldn't have known," Carina said.

"Yes, I could have. All I had to do was

259

ask instead of jumping to the worst possible conclusion."

"Honey, after what you've been through, no one can blame you."

"I can," I said. "And I'm pretty sure that he does too. I don't think he's ever coming back. I've lost the best man I've ever known." Tears welled up in my eyes. "Maybe the best thing I've ever known."

"This is my fault," Carina said. "I should have just stayed out of it."

I put my head in my hands. When I could speak, I said, "What do I do?"

"You need to go to him."

"What if he won't see me?"

"I don't know. I guess we'll jump off that bridge when we come to it."

CHAPTER
Thirty-Seven

There is nothing more predictable than
the law of the harvest. I'm reaping the
pain of the hurt I've sowed.
—Maggie Walther's Diary

It was after dark on Friday night when I drove
back to the Christmas tree lot. As much as I had
replayed our conversation, I still really didn't
know what I would say to him when I saw him.
Truthfully, I think I would have said anything to
make him like me again.

I had previously been to Andrew's lot only
during the day; in the evening it was much busier
than I had ever seen it. The parking lot was
full, and I ended up parking at a drive-in across
the street and walking over. The place looked
different. The strands of Christmas lights that
were strung above the lot were lit, and Christmas
music played over a PA system. Everything felt
more alive but me.

I looked up and down the rows of trees looking
for Andrew. Twice my heart leapt when I thought
I saw him, but both times it just turned out to be
another customer.

I had walked the entire lot twice when I finally

stopped Shelby, who was busy helping someone.

"Excuse me," I said.

"I'll be right with you, ma'am," Shelby said, then he recognized me. "Oh, hey. It's you." The woman he was helping glared at me as if I had just jumped a line.

"I'm looking for Andrew. Is he here?"

"Negatory. He never works weekends."

Of course, I thought. It was Friday. "So he'll be back Monday?"

"Ah, not sure about that." He shouted to someone I couldn't see. "Hey, Chris, when is the boss back?"

"Eighteenth," came the reply.

"Oh, gotcha, dude." He turned back to me. "Yeah, he's gonna be gone a while. Like until the eighteenth."

My heart fell. That was more than two weeks away.

"Excuse me," the customer said. "I'll take this tree."

"Gotcha," Shelby said without looking at her. He continued, "So, the boss was, like, kinda noncommittal, you know what I mean? He said, like, maybe the eighteenth, but then, like, maybe not. I think it depends on how things go down. I heard his brother's getting out of jail, and he's gonna spend some time with him, get him readjusted to life outside, you know what I mean?"

"I know what you mean," I said. I breathed out heavily. "All right. Would you please tell him I came by?"

"Gotcha," he said, then added, "I can go one better. If you give me your number, I'll text you when he's back."

I wasn't sure that he wasn't just trying to get my phone number, but it was worth the risk. I gave it to him and he dialed it into his phone. "Gotcha," he said, which by now I figured was his catchphrase. "Oh, wait. I need to put your name on this. What's your name?"

"It's Maggie," I said.

"I won't remember that. I'll just put Stacy's Mom. That's what Chris calls you. You know, like that song."

"Gotcha," I said. I walked back to my car, dragging my heart behind me.

CHAPTER
Thirty-Eight

Clive may have tied his noose with my heartstrings, but that doesn't mean I have to attend the hanging.
—Maggie Walther's Diary

The next two weeks were miserable. It snowed, of course. I had given up complaining about it. In a way, that was true about my life as well.

It literally took me most of a day to get up the nerve to call Andrew. He didn't answer, nor did he return my messages. I sent about a dozen texts before I accepted that I was just making myself look pathetic. For the first time, I was starting to believe that he really was done with me. I shouldn't have been surprised. That's what happens when you handle someone's heart carelessly.

On December ninth I thought about him all day. (Who am I kidding? I thought about him all day, every day.) According to our last conversation, that was the day his brother was to be paroled. I wondered what that would be like for him. I wondered if he had ever told his brother about me.

On the home front, I couldn't stand the isolation

anymore and went back to work. Carina had done a good job taking care of the clients but not the business. It wasn't her fault. She had never been trained to run the place, nor did she have the authority to pay bills. Our Internet service had been canceled, and we were just two days away from the power company turning off the kitchen's electricity.

I worked at the bakery but none of the events. I still felt uncomfortable in public. Besides, there was enough to keep me busy with baking and preparation, let alone catching up with the business side of the company. I was glad when Carina stopped asking if I had heard from Andrew.

Tuesday night, the thirteenth, as I was getting ready for bed, Clive paid me a visit. He had probably lost twenty pounds, and his clothes, which looked like they hadn't been ironed in weeks, hung on him. He looked like an underfed scarecrow. In spite of everything, I felt sorry for him.

"May I come in?" he asked humbly.

"Yes." I stepped aside and he walked in. "Are you hungry?"

"No. You wouldn't have any vodka, would you?"

"I've got apple juice."

"Close enough," he said.

I poured him a glass of juice, and he sat

down at the kitchen table. "In light of, recent revelations"—that was his way of saying the discovery of another wife without actually saying it—"the prosecution has decided to move the court date to January sixth."

"Have you pled yet?"

"My second arraignment was last week."

"What did you plead?"

"Same as the first time. Not guilty."

"But you are."

"It's a strategy. Once you plead guilty, you have no leverage." His eyes looked hollow. "With all the media attention, the prosecution is grandstanding. They're pushing to put me behind bars. I could do up to five years."

I looked at him sadly. "Are there more, Clive?"

"More women?"

I nodded. He looked down. "No other wives." Then he softly added, "There's a woman in San Diego. We weren't married . . ."

I shook my head in disbelief. "Why, Clive? We had such a good life. Why wasn't I enough?"

"I've been trying to figure that out myself. Yesterday, I read something on the mating rituals of primates. It said that once a male chimpanzee establishes his alpha position, he immediately starts collecting a harem. He can't help it. It's hardwired into the male's psyche for the protection and growth of the species."

"I wouldn't use that argument in court," I said.

He took a slow drink of juice, then rolled the cup between his hands as though he were thinking. He looked at me and asked, "Do you still love me?"

Sadly—or tellingly—I wondered if he had asked that to set me up for a request. Finally, I answered, "I loved the man I married. More than you know."

He looked like he didn't know what to do with that.

"Is that why you came, Clive? To ask me that?"

He scratched his forehead. "No. I came to tell you that I'm sorry. You were the best thing in my life. I didn't know it then, but I do now. It took me some time to figure that out. Too much time. A day late and a dollar short, right?"

"Nine years late," I said.

"Yeah." He stood. "At least." He exhaled. "I just wanted you to know that. Take care of yourself, Mag." He started toward the door, then stopped. "By the way, how's it going with that guy you're dating?"

I don't know why he asked me that. I don't know why I answered him. "He's gone."

"Is that your doing or his?"

"It was his."

"Then he's a fool."

"He's not a fool."

"Anyone who gives you up is a fool." He stepped outside, then turned back and said, "I've got someone coming to replace your window tomorrow afternoon. I hope that works for you."

"Thank you."

"Don't mention it." He turned and walked away.

CHAPTER
Thirty-Nine

He came. *He.* I don't even know his name anymore.

—Maggie Walther's Diary

The next night there was an ambulance in the Stephenses' driveway. I walked out onto my front porch to see Mrs. Stephens being wheeled out on a gurney, with Mr. Stephens walking at her side.

It turned out that she had suffered a stroke. I planned to visit her in the hospital but never got the chance. She suffered a second stroke the next morning and passed away.

Saturday night I went to her viewing at a nearby Mormon chapel. Mr. Stephens was completely bereft, standing next to his wife's casket. He had lost the whole of his family in just one winter. I hated this winter.

In spite of his grief, Mr. Stephens seemed glad to see me. "First my son, then my wife," he said. "Leisa *was* my life. Why couldn't it have been me?"

We cried together. I think that's what love should be.

Every day I thought about Andrew. I kept hoping I would hear from him when he got back, if not sooner. The eighteenth came and went. I drove by the lot several times but didn't see his truck. I felt like a stalker. Maybe I *was* a stalker. Why couldn't I just accept that it was over? I guess because, for me, it wasn't over. I needed something more definite. I needed an axe to fall on something. Maybe my heart.

Around noon on the twentieth I received a text message from an unfamiliar number. All it said was,

555-5964
Boss is back

It was from Shelby. The hipster had actually come through. I drove immediately over to the Christmas tree lot. It was different from the last time I'd been there. The parking lot was nearly empty, and Andrew's truck sat up front near the trailer. I parked my little Fiat next to it, took a deep breath, said a mantra three times— *If you give fear legs, it will run away with your dreams*—and then walked into the lot.

There was only one customer, and Andrew was helping him at the trailer. I stood at a distance, waiting for him to leave. Then Andrew saw me. He glanced up at me, then turned away nearly as quickly.

He finished the transaction. As the customer was leaving, I walked up to him, our eyes locked on each other. When I got close, he said, "What do you want, Maggie?"

"You," I said.

He didn't say anything, which made my heart feel like a truck had parked on it. He just stood there.

"Wow," I said, more to myself than him, "you really are done with me." My eyes welled. I looked at him, fighting back the weight of his rejection. I finally said, "Before I go, would you do me just one kindness?"

"What's that?" he asked.

"Tell me that you don't have any feelings for me—that everything you once felt is gone." I wiped my cheek. "I need to hear it. It's the only way I can start to move on."

He looked down for a moment, then said, "I can't, Maggie. It wouldn't be true."

"Then why are you torturing me?"

His brow furrowed. "Why can't you see that I'm protecting you?"

"From what?"

"From *me*."

"I don't want to be protected from you. I don't care what you've done, or what your brother did. None of that matters to me."

He looked even more upset. Actually, he looked lost. He raked his hand through his hair. Then he said, "All right. I get off in an hour. We'll talk."

"Do you want me to wait?"

"No. I'll come over to your place."

"Thank you," I said softly.

"Don't thank me," he said.

I drove home with my chest aching. There was a fierce battle going on inside between fear and hope. I'm not sure which was more dangerous.

CHAPTER
Forty

He came. He. I don't even know his name anymore.

—Maggie Walther's Diary

Andrew arrived at my house ninety minutes later, half an hour later than I'd expected. The extra thirty minutes felt like days. I wondered if he had changed his mind.

I met him at the door and let him in. This time he hugged me. I didn't know what kind of hug it was, one of love or condolence, but I wasn't picky. I was just glad to feel him. We sat down together on the couch—the same couch where he had comforted me and I had first fallen in love with him. Same couch, different world.

For a moment we sat in awkward silence, not sure how to begin. Then I said, "May I go first?"

He nodded.

My voice was soft and strained. I couldn't look at him as I spoke. "Andrew, I love you. I know I really screwed up and I don't deserve you, but I'm just hoping that you can somehow forgive me and give me a chance to show you how much I love you." A tear fell down my cheek. "My heart is broken." He still didn't speak. I looked up into his eyes. "Do you care that it's broken?"

His eyes welled up. Then he shook his head. "You're right, you don't deserve me. But not in the way you think." He gave a heavy sigh. "It's time you knew the truth." He pulled back slightly, squaring himself to me. "Of course I care that your heart's broken. My heart's broken too. But that doesn't change reality. What you need—what you really deserve—is the truth. And the truth is, you don't know who I am." He looked me in the eyes. "Maggie, I can't fake it anymore. I love you too much for that."

I took his hand. "I know who you are. You're the man who held me when my world was falling apart. You're the man who takes food to the poor. I know you. I know you're good and generous and kind. What more do I need to know?"

"A lot," he said softly.

"Tell me, then. What am I missing?"

He was quiet for a long time. Then he looked into my eyes and said, "Ask me my name."

I just looked at him.

"Ask me my name, Maggie."

I had no idea why he was asking me to do that, but something in the way he said it frightened me. I swallowed. "What is your name?"

"My name is Aaron Hill."

I just looked at him. "I don't understand."

"Andrew is my brother. I'm Aaron. I'm the one

who stole millions of my clients' dollars. Not my brother."

"But your brother went to prison."

"I took the money, but my brother took the time. He went to prison in my place."

His words took a moment to sink in. "I don't believe you."

"You don't believe me, or you don't want to believe me?"

"Either."

"What would you have me do to convince you?"

"Tell me what happened."

He rubbed his chin. "All right." He took a moment to gather his thoughts. "I told you about the trial. It lasted almost two weeks. Most of it was technical, the state laying out exactly where the money had gone, how many illegal transactions had actually been made, all my criminal details. They didn't have to work for the information, since I provided them with most of it. You could say I helped build my gallows.

"It was the worst time of my life. It was as difficult as when my parents died. In some ways, worse. There was no shame with my parents' death.

"Every day I thought of taking my life. Several times I planned it out in detail. Every day I fought that battle by myself. I was completely alone. My friends, or at least the people I thought were my friends, deserted me. My cheating wife had already divorced me and was using my weakened position to make false accusations of abuse, hoping to take everything I had." He looked at me with despair. "Kick them when they're down, right?"

"What about your brother? Where was he?"

Aaron shook his head. "I hadn't seen Andrew since he helped boot me out of my own company."

"Your brother was involved with that?"

Aaron nodded slowly, and I could see that it still hurt him. "It couldn't have happened without him. Together we owned the majority of the stock. It wasn't his idea, but he made it possible. The truth is, the investors played him. But he went along." He slowly exhaled in anguish. "It's like I said: I was betrayed by *everyone*."

I just looked at him with pity.

"It was the morning of what was likely the last day of my trial. I had hardly slept, and when I got out of bed, I was so anxious that I threw up. I was literally counting down my last minutes of freedom, anticipating the fear and humiliation of life in prison. I can't begin to describe what that was like. I'd been on trial for almost two weeks by then, and all that was left were the attorneys' closing arguments and the jury's deliberation.

"The trial hadn't gone well." He smiled darkly. "That's an understatement. To begin with, I had already confessed to the crime, so I had no leverage. Nothing to bargain with."

I remembered what Clive told me the other evening about not pleading guilty.

"There was no doubt that I was going to prison. The only question was for how long. So there I was, numb and nauseated, my mind spinning like a top, wondering how long it would be before I saw my house again. I felt crazy, like I was losing my mind.

"Then, in the midst of that insane moment, Andrew walked into my house. Not exactly someone I wanted to see. Part of me wanted to punch him, but the fact was, I didn't have any fight left in me. I asked him if he'd come to gloat or to steal. He said he came to talk. I said there was nothing left to talk about and no time to do it. I told him my lawyer would be there any minute to take me to court. He said, 'I know. That's why I'm here.'

"I said, 'I'm going to prison, brother. I hope that makes you and your cronies happy.' I took out my wallet and offered him a hundred-dollar bill. 'Here, buy some champagne and have a toast on me. To your felon brother. May he rot in prison.'

"He just looked at me and said, 'You're not going to prison.'

"I said, 'You clearly haven't been following my trial.' Just then my lawyer honked his horn outside. I said, 'That's my ride. Lock up after yourself.'

"I started to leave, but he said, 'I've been following your trial, Aaron. You're not going to prison, because I am.' Then he set his driver's license and keys on my counter, along with a small leather book. 'I've put everything in order. These are the keys to my car and house. The house alarm number is the last four digits of your phone number. This notebook has every bank account, username, password, and code I have. It's all yours. There's a wall safe behind the floral painting in my bedroom. The combination to it is in the book. Inside the safe are keys to my safe deposit boxes and the Cabo condo. Everything else you can figure out.'

" 'What are you doing?' I asked.

"He said, 'I'm taking your place. I'm going to leave with your lawyer, and you're going to take my car and drive to my home and start a new life with my name. Now give me your driver's license.'

"I couldn't believe what he was saying. I told him, 'You can't do this.'

"His eyes welled up. 'I *have* to do this,' he said. 'I helped them betray you. You never would have gotten caught up in any of this if it wasn't for what I let them do to you.'

"I said, 'I'm not going to let you.'

"He looked at me and said, 'I figured you would

probably say that. So I'm going to lay out your options. You can give me your license and let me do this, or you can go to prison while I go home and wait for the verdict. If you're given anything besides probation, I'll blow my head off with that Smith & Wesson you gave me for my twenty-fifth birthday.' He stared me in the eye. 'Believe it or not, I actually do have a conscience. I can't live with what I've done. Guilt is its own kind of prison. It's what hell is made of.

" 'Sorry to spring this on you, brother, but those are your options. You let me go to prison for a few years and attempt to make amends and assuage my guilt, or you go to prison with the knowledge that you killed your brother. That shouldn't be too hard a decision.' He held out his hand. 'Now hurry and give me your license. I'm assuming my lawyer charges by the hour.'

"I took out my wallet and gave him my driver's license. He said, 'You might as well give me the whole wallet, because after today, Aaron Hill doesn't exist outside of prison.'

"As I handed him my wallet, my cell phone rang. It was my lawyer. Andrew said, 'I should take that too.' He handed me his phone as he answered mine, saying he would be right out. Then he looked at me and said, 'I'm sorry for what I did to you. I hope this will help you forgive me.' He began to turn, then stopped and said, 'One more thing: I didn't know Scott was cheating with Jamie. I would have prevented that if I could have. I would have told you. I'm not that despicable.' I thanked him. He said, 'Thank you for letting me do this. I'll see you in a couple of years.' Then he put on his sunglasses, walked out of my house, and drove away with my attorney.

"I went down to the courthouse to watch the rest of the trial. It was maddening seeing the prosecution paint me as a monster and watching my brother take it. When the jury pronounced their verdict, Andrew didn't even flinch. After the gavel came down, my brother looked back and made eye contact with me. Then he nodded slightly and turned. The officer handcuffed him and took him away."

He took a deep breath. "My brother gave me his name. For the last two years I've lived as Andrew Hill." He looked at me. "He's out now. He's still in Colorado for the time being—but not as a convicted felon. I've given him his name back. He's Andrew again. And I'm Aaron, the ex-convict with a record."

I let the pronouncement settle. Then I said, "What if I told you that I love you no matter what you've done or what your name is?"

"I would say you're a fool." He leaned forward and kissed me on the cheek. "Good-bye, Maggie."

"Where are you going?"

"Someplace where bad things never happen."

CHAPTER
Forty-One

Today I had the most unexpected of visitors with the most unexpected of stories.
—Maggie Walther's Diary

The commercial world of Christmas kept me busy. There were parties everywhere, and my company catered more than its share of them—sometimes up to three events a day.

I had already abandoned my plans to go back home to Oregon, cataloging the idea in the "What was I thinking?" file. I suppose it's evidence of just how desperate I was to get away from my situation—like a coyote chewing off its leg to escape a trap.

I kept thinking how glad I would be when this year was over. These, no doubt, were days I would never forget, but I wanted to. Let's just say I was looking forward to looking back on them.

With all the business, I was able to keep myself distracted. I was grateful for that. But that's all it was: a distraction. You can throw a blanket over something you don't want to see, but it's still there.

I wondered where he was. I wondered how long it would be before I stopped thinking about him every day and could let him go. Apparently, that's not what fate had in mind. My story still had one last twist.

It was a few days before Christmas. I had just returned home from catering a redneck wedding dinner that drew moments from *The Twilight Zone*—like when the drunk, obviously pregnant bride started yelling at her husband of six hours that he was ruining the day because he was more drunk than she was. Then one of the wedding guests loudly complained because we weren't serving fried chicken and corn on the cob. I told her that the bride hadn't ordered fried chicken and corn on the cob. The guest replied that that wasn't her problem and asked what I planned to do about it. I told her there was a KFC just a few blocks away and I'd be happy to draw her a map.

As I was pulling into my driveway, I noticed a red, expensive-looking sports car idling in front of my house. I'm not an expert on cars, but I'm pretty sure it was a Ferrari. I wondered who it belonged to and why it was parked in front of my house.

I pulled into the garage and shut the door behind me. Then, as I walked into my house, the doorbell rang. I walked to the front door. After the brick incident, I'd had a peephole installed by the same people who replaced my window. I looked through it to see who was there. It was Aaron.

I fumbled madly with the lock and dead bolt

and swung open the door. The excitement on my face must have been pretty obvious, because the man raised a hand and said, "I'm not who you think I am."

I stopped, confused.

He stepped closer to me. "You're Maggie, right? I'm Aaron's brother, Andrew."

He looked exactly like his brother. He looked exactly like the man I loved.

"Come in," I said.

He stepped into my living room. Even his mannerisms were the same as Aaron's. I motioned to the couch. "Have a seat."

"Thank you."

I sat down in the armchair across from him. Andrew glanced at my Christmas tree and sat down. "Nice tree."

"Andrew and I . . ." I caught myself. "*Aaron* and I decorated it. It was from his Christmas tree lot."

"I thought it was a little strange that he got into that business. But if anyone can figure out how to make money selling Christmas trees, it's him."

Every time he looked at me I felt peculiar, as though it was him but also wasn't. It's like the time I made banana bread and someone had filled the sugar canister with salt. The bread looked the same, but it wasn't. Finally, I said, "I'm sorry; this is . . . surreal. You and your brother look exactly alike."

"Actually, I'm more buff than he is these days," Andrew said. "I've had more time to work out in the gym lately."

"Speaking of which," I said, "how are you?"

"I'm out," he said. "Out is good. Free is good."

"I can't believe you would do what you did for your brother."

"That's why I came to talk to you. If you knew how much he'd done for me, you wouldn't be surprised. He was always looking out for me. And being a twin added another dimension to that."

"What do you mean?"

"Like, when I was in middle school, I desperately wanted to play on the school basketball team. I wasn't a Jordan or a LeBron, but I had talent. I practiced every day to get ready for tryouts. The day tryouts began, some random kid at lunch thought it would be funny to drop a bowl of chili on my head. I broke his nose. Not surprisingly, I was sent to the principal's office. The principal assigned me detention every night after school for the next two weeks. I told him I had basketball tryouts. He said, 'You should have thought about that before you punched that boy.'

"There was nothing I could do about it. I could skip detention, but then I'd be suspended and wouldn't be allowed to play anyway.

"After school I went to the library for detention. When I arrived, Aaron was already there. He had checked in under my name. He just looked at me and nodded. I went to tryouts and made the team. I needed that right then, and Aaron knew it. He always had my back.

"Unfortunately—mostly for me—our genetic duplication only went as far as our appearance. Personality-wise, we were salt and pepper. He was the salt; I was the pepper. I was impetuous; he was methodical. I was careless; he was disciplined. I got in fights; Aaron talked people out of them.

"Mostly, he had more smarts than anyone I'd ever known. He was the brains behind everything we did. I learned to just follow along, because he knew what he was doing; if I couldn't keep up, he would pick up the slack. I even got an MBA because he did. Except while he was at home studying, I'd be out partying.

"My last year I had a final in global economics. The class was a nightmare. The professor was one of those bitter, arrogant types who treated his students like dirt, then rationalized his cruelty as 'teaching moments.' I hated the guy almost as much as I hated the class. I just couldn't get into it. I didn't care enough to get into it.

"The day before the final, I took a practice exam to see how I would do. I failed it miserably. I knew I couldn't pass the test. And if I didn't pass it, I wouldn't graduate.

"That night, instead of studying, I went out

and partied all night. I woke the next day at noon with a wicked hangover. Not that it would have made much of a difference, but by the time I remembered the exam, I had missed it.

"I was embarrassed to tell Aaron. I hated letting him down. A couple of hours later, when he got home, I said, 'I missed the test.' He handed me my student ID and said, 'No, you passed it. Now earn it.' That's the way it's always been.

"When we started our company, I knew I was just riding his coattails, but I was okay with that. I mean, it had always been that way, and it beat punching a clock somewhere. Besides, I was more social and Aaron was more focused on work, so it was kind of a symbiotic relationship. Aaron never once treated me like I was a burden.

"He would bring in these super-wealthy investors, the kind of guys who could drop ten grand on a roulette wheel and not lose any sleep over it. Aaron took their money and made them richer. He was on fire, making all the right decisions, all the right acquisitions. He made just one mistake: he didn't take credit for what he did. He was too absorbed in succeeding to tell everyone about his success. I once had a professor tell me, 'In business, sometimes it's better to look good than to be good.' There may be some truth to that.

"So when the partners got greedy, they didn't know I wasn't making the same contribution

Aaron was. Most of the time they didn't even know which of us was which. They just knew Aaron was taking the largest piece of the pie, and they wanted it.

"They couldn't make a move without me, since Aaron and I held the majority of the shares, but with my percentage, they could control everything. So they wined and dined me. They didn't tell me they wanted Aaron out; they just flattered me by saying I should be the managing partner and offered me a rock-star salary and full ownership of the condominium in Cabo San Lucas. The one you stayed at.

"The truth was, it wasn't the swag I fell for, it was their flattery. I wanted to believe that I was as good as my brother. I wanted to show Aaron that I was more than just his slacker twin.

"So, with my help, they took control. To my everlasting regret, they immediately pushed Aaron out of the company he had started." Andrew shook his head. "I'll never forget Aaron's face when they told him. We were all gathered around the conference room table, but it was like no one else was in the room, just him and me. The whole time, Aaron just stared at me in disbelief.

"The vultures did give me the raise they said they would; they just hadn't told me it would come from my brother's paycheck.

"Aaron was devastated. Of course he was. I

had betrayed him. And if that wasn't bad enough, the next week his wife, Jamie, informed him that she had been having an affair with one of the investors and wanted a divorce. I think that's when he snapped. He had lost his company and his wife. But the biggest hurt, I think, still came from my betrayal.

"Broken or not, Aaron was no quitter. Within a month he had started a new firm. It had the same business model, the same plan; the only difference was him. He was drinking heavily. He wasn't careful. He wasn't confident. Then, when some of his early investments didn't pan out, he went off the rails.

"Rather than accept failure, he started taking his investors' money and hiding it. I don't know what his end game was—maybe he was planning to disappear off the grid—but we never found out. He couldn't go through with it.

"After he turned himself in, I watched him self-destruct. He had lost everything: his reputation, his company, his wife, his family—and, worst of all, his self-respect. Thankfully he cooperated with the authorities. That's why he got only a couple of years. A couple of years that I owed him."

I let the story sink in. My heart ached for Aaron and what he'd been through, but in light of our situation, it seemed moot. "Why are you telling me this? Aaron and I aren't together anymore."

"That's precisely why I'm telling you this. My brother visited me every week for those two years. Even after he moved to Utah. He would drive ten hours each way just so we could talk for an hour. I'd wait all week for that hour. It's what got me through.

"It didn't matter what we talked about. We'd usually start out discussing the latest headlines or sports, the Nuggets or Broncos, but we'd always end up talking business and some opportunities we could possibly pursue once I got out. Just like old times. Between the lines, he was assuring me that he had forgiven me. And he was leaving me with hope."

He smiled. "And then, one day, you entered the mix. After that, you were all he wanted to talk about. I was the one who suggested he take you to Cabo. When he came back from that trip, he told me he had found the woman he wanted to spend the rest of his life with."

"But then he left me."

"For a reason. It's because, in the same way he watched out for me, he was watching out for you. He doesn't want the woman he loves to live with a broken man. It's that simple. He left you because he loved you."

"That doesn't make sense."

"Maybe not to most people, but it does to him. Some people love for what they can get. A rare few, like Aaron, love for what they can give.

The measure of love isn't how much you want someone. It's revealed in what you want *for* them. He wanted you to have something better than life with a felon."

"But he knew he was a felon when we met."

Andrew nodded. "I know. This is where it gets a bit hazy for me too. But I'm pretty sure that my release from prison complicated things. I think, on some subconscious level, he could function as Andrew. But after he gave me my name back, he was Aaron the disgraced businessman. Aaron the felon." He shook his head. "Names are powerful things."

I just sat there quietly thinking. Then I said, "What do you think I should do?"

"That depends on what you want. Do you know what you want?"

I nodded. "I want him."

He looked at me intensely. "Are you sure?"

"Absolutely."

"Then go get him."

"But I don't even know where he is."

A knowing smile crossed Andrew's face. "Of course you do."

CHAPTER
Forty-Two

Sometimes love requires us to leap and just hope that there's someone there to catch us.

—Maggie Walther's Diary

My flight touched down in Los Cabos shortly before eleven on Christmas morning. I had hired an English-speaking Uber driver to take me to Todos Santos. He was a forty-year-old immigrant from Ukraine named Kostya, who claimed he spoke better English than Spanish.

I met my driver in the terminal. He was holding a piece of cardboard with my name written on it. He grabbed my bag, then asked me for the name of the hotel in Todos Santos I was staying at. I told him I didn't even have an address. We talked the whole ride about life in Mexico. He asked me how long I was staying. I told him I had no idea.

Kostya left the highway a few miles past the Todos Santos town sign. At my instruction, he turned down a short dirt road, then drove up onto the sandy beach. There was the house Aaron had shown me, except the For Sale sign was gone.

He drove to within thirty yards of the coral-pink structure and stopped. "Is this good, Mag-gie?"

"Yes. Thank you." I paid him in pesos I'd exchanged my dollars for at the airport. Then I gave him a hundred-dollar tip for Christmas. He was beyond happy. We got out of his car and he lifted my bag out of the trunk.

"Mag-gie, do you want me to wait?" he asked.

"Yes, please. I'd better make sure he's here."

The pink stucco home glowed brilliantly against the blue ocean backdrop. Palm trees surrounded the house; some of the shorter ones were wrapped with Christmas lights. A rope hammock had been tied between two of the trees. It rocked, unoccupied, in the wind.

As far as I could see, the only signs of occupancy were a motorcycle parked to the side of the house and clothes hanging on a line, rippling like flags in the ocean breeze. I recognized one of Aaron's shirts from our trip together.

I walked up onto the front porch and knocked on the door, but there was no answer. I tried the doorknob. It was unlocked, so I opened the door and looked inside. "Aaron?" The room inside was clean and spacious but showed no sign of anyone living there.

I walked around the side of the house. The back of the property was neatly landscaped with palm trees, cactus, and terra-cotta-potted kumquat trees set on beige slate pavers surrounding a bright-blue brick-and-mosaic-tile-lined swimming pool.

The property continued on about a hundred feet down to the ocean, with a wooden dock extending out over the water. A fishing boat was secured to the end of the dock. *What had he called it?* I couldn't remember its Spanish name, but I remembered the translation, because I remembered thinking, *How appropriate. The Dream.*

As I neared the dock, mixed with the sound of seagulls and crashing waves, I could hear music. Seventies music. Supertramp. "Goodbye Stranger." Aaron had to be there.

I turned and waved to Kostya, who was sitting on the hood of his car smoking a cigarette. He waved back, got into his car, and drove away.

Then I walked out onto the dock. In the distance, a line of pelicans roller-coastered past the beach. As I approached, I could see that a new name had been painted on the boat.

AGNETHA

Then I saw him. I'm not exactly sure what he was doing; he was facing the sea, kneeling on the boat's hull, sanding or polishing. He wasn't wearing a shirt or shoes, just a black, boxy bathing suit.

I had almost reached the end of the dock when he suddenly turned back as if he'd sensed someone's presence. For a moment he just looked at me. Then he tossed aside whatever was in his hand, jumped down onto the dock, and started toward me.

He was tan, his hair mussed as if it hadn't been combed for a while. I couldn't tell if he was more shocked or awed. When he got to me, he just said, "Hi."

"Hi," I said back.

"What are you doing here?"

"I came to wish you a merry Christmas."

"You could have just texted."

"You don't answer my texts. And besides, I had something to ask you."

"What's that?"

"At my house I said, 'What if I told you that I love you no matter what you've done or what your name is?' And you answered, 'I would say you're a fool.' Do you remember?"

He nodded. "It was something like that."

"It was exactly like that," I said. "I had a follow-up question."

"Okay."

"What do you have against fools?"

A large smile crossed his face.

"So here's the deal, Mr. Hill. I want you. I want to explore life with you. I want to experience life with you. I want to battle life with you." I lifted my arms and flexed. "I can do it. I'm pretty strong."

"I have no doubt," he said.

"So what will it be? Am I staying, or am I going back to Cabo tonight?"

"That depends on how long you were planning on staying."

Suddenly the lightness left my heart. I looked at him seriously and asked, "How long will you let me stay?"

His voice and demeanor also took on a more serious tone. He looked deep into my eyes. "How about forever?"

I just looked at him for a second, then rushed into him and we kissed. After we had kissed for a minute, I started laughing.

"What's so funny?" he asked, still trying to kiss me.

"It's good you said that."

"Why is that?"

"I already sent my car back."

Then we really kissed. Soulfully, passionately, joyfully. And the sea and beach and sun all witnessed and applauded our happiness in their own ways. Sometime later (a long time later) when we came up for air, I whispered, "I love you, Aaron Hill."

"I love you, Agnetha."

I smiled. "Merry Christmas, my stranger."

"Merry Christmas, my love," he whispered back. "Welcome to forever."

EPILOGUE

For far too long, all I saw was the night, forgetting that the sun must set if it is to rise again.
　　　　　　　　　—Maggie Walther's Diary

Mi español está mejorándose. My Spanish is getting pretty good. At least I can order a coffee and concha and find a bathroom. What else really matters?

Aaron and I have breakfast or coffee every morning outside on the porch, with the cool Pacific breeze dancing in our hair. Sometimes I go out fishing with him, but not often. I'm still afraid to go into deep waters on account of his Humboldt squid story. One night at a Todos Santos pub a man lifted his shirt and showed us his scar from a Humboldt bite. It was horrific.

Aaron and I were married on November 10, 2017—a year to the day after we met at Aaron's Christmas tree lot. The marriage was performed by a local minister. I'd always wanted a beach wedding. Carina was my maid of honor. Andrew was Aaron's best man. I was hoping to hook the two of them up, but it just wasn't there. Sometimes the magic happens, sometimes it doesn't. There's no rhyme or reason to love.

Life is slower here. More deliberate. We have time together. We sleep in, make love, take long walks on the beach—pretty much all the things dreams are made of.

I gave Carina ownership of Just Desserts, passing it on just as Marge had done with me. But my entrepreneurial drive is still intact. I'm opening a bakery in town, and already have contracts with several local resorts.

Clive had his day in court. He was fined ten thousand dollars and ordered to perform two hundred hours of community service. No jail time. Some people thought he got off easy, but I don't. He was given a life sentence when he lost his dreams and political aspirations. And me.

Aaron continues to manage his investments, but lately, most of the time he works on his book. It's almost done. It's pretty good, really. It's about a twin who goes to prison for his brother. I'd always wondered how authors came up with their ideas.

I still slip up sometimes and call him Andrew. Whenever I do, he threatens to change his name to a glyph that has no pronunciation, like Prince did. I just tell him it will get in the way of his publishing career and maybe even our love life, and he quickly retreats.

We've continued the Thanksgiving tradition, though our list of recipients just keeps getting longer.

Andrew—the real Andrew—moved to Connecticut. He now has a fiancée. Her name is Emma. She's lovely. They visit often, though they usually stay in Andrew's condo in Cabo. Whenever they come, the brothers take a cooler with some fruit, a couple of six-packs, a loaf of bread, and a couple of chorizo sausages and go out on the *Agnetha*. What is it with men and boats?

Our love continues to grow. So does our happiness. That's how it's supposed to be, right? Our love is also growing in other ways: I'm five months pregnant with a little girl. We plan to name her Marissa, which means "of the sea." Marissa Hill. We still haven't decided whether we'll raise her here. I'll guess we'll see. We've got a few years before school starts.

Time rolls on. When I think back on all that happened that year, I'm still amazed that we survived it all. But that's what we do. That's what life and love require of us—to walk on in spite of the "slings and arrows of outrageous fortune," to walk on and hold to love. If we do that, we may suffer for a time, but we will not fail. In the end, love wins. It reminds me of a Mexican proverb that describes us perfectly: *Quisieron enterrarnos, pero se les olvidó que somos semillas.* It means, "They tried to bury us. They just didn't know we were seeds."

ACKNOWLEDGMENTS

I'd like to acknowledge and thank my Simon & Schuster friends, especially Carolyn Reidy and Jonathan Karp, for their continued friendship and support of my writing. To my new editor, Amar Deol, I look forward to working on more books with you. Continued love and appreciation to my agent, Laurie Liss, and my staff: Jenna Evans Welch, Barry Evans, Heather McVey, and Diane Glad. Also, to all my brothers in the Tribe of Kyngs.

Appreciation to award-winning producer Norman Stephens; it's been such a pleasure working with you on all those movies. (I'm so glad your wife found me.)

Most of all, to my sweet wife, Keri. This book is for you.

ABOUT THE AUTHOR

Richard Paul Evans is the #1 bestselling author of *The Christmas Box* and the *Michael Vey* series. Each of his more than thirty-five novels has been a *New York Times* bestseller. There are more than thirty million copies of his books in print worldwide, translated into more than twenty-four languages. He is the recipient of numerous awards, including the American Mothers Book Award, the *Romantic Times* Best Women's Novel of the Year Award, the German Audience Gold Award for Romance, four Religion Communicators Council Wilbur Awards, the Washington Times Humanitarian of the Century Award, and the Volunteers of America Empathy Award. He lives in Salt Lake City, Utah, with his wife, Keri, not far from their five children and two grandchildren. You can learn more about Richard on Facebook at www.facebook.com/RPEfans or read his blog at www.richardpaulevans.com.

Books are produced in the United States using U.S.-based materials

Books are printed using a revolutionary new process called THINKtech™ that lowers energy usage by 70% and increases overall quality

Books are durable and flexible because of Smyth-sewing

Paper is sourced using environmentally responsible foresting methods and the paper is acid-free

Center Point Large Print
600 Brooks Road / PO Box 1
Thorndike, ME 04986-0001 USA

(207) 568-3717

US & Canada:
1 800 929-9108
www.centerpointlargeprint.com